Caught on a Train

Also by Carlo Gébler

Frozen Out

For younger readers

The Base

Caught on a Train

Carlo Gébler

mammoth

With thanks to 'The Oriental and Tribal Specialist',
Neal Street East in Covent Garden, London
for the loan of the Tibetan slippers
which appear in the front cover illustration.

First published in Great Britain 2001 by Mammoth,
an imprint of Egmont Children's Books Limited,
a division of Egmont Holding Limited
239 Kensington High Street, London W8 6SA

Text copyright © 2001 Carlo Gébler
Cover illustration copyright © 2001 Stuart Haygarth

The moral rights of the author and cover illustrator
have been asserted.

ISBN 0 7497 4623 8

10 9 8 7 6 5 4 3 2

A CIP catalogue record for this title is available from the
British Library

Typeset by Avon DataSet Ltd, Bidford on Avon, B50 4JH
(www.avondataset.com)
Printed in Great Britain by Cox & Wyman Ltd, Reading,
Berkshire

For India, Jack, Finn
Georgia & Euan

I gratefully acknowledge the financial support of
the Arts Council/An Chomhairle Ealaíon

Author's note

The stories retold here have been told before and will doubtless be retold again. The versions of 'Soul Cages' and 'Daniel O'Rourke' that I found most helpful were those written up by the Irish antiquary, Thomas Crofton Croker; 'Bewitched Butter,' was published in the *Dublin University Magazine*, 1839, but no author was credited. All three works are gathered in W B Yeats's excellent anthology, *Irish Fairy & Folk Tales*. All inventions and additions are my own.

Carlo Gébler

Contents

Something wicked this way comes
   For old Nick's a-stirring
Something wicked this way comes
   He'll have your soul for burning.

Victorian song, anon

Part One

The Train

Let me tell you of the December day in 1899, sixty years ago, I can never, ever, forget . . .

I was fourteen. We had no money. We couldn't afford our own clock. So when I got the job on the railways, my mother asked Pat Sweeney, the local knocker-up, to wake me every morning at four o'clock. She had to pay him an ha'penny a week.

The knocker had a stick with a bit of metal on the end. He came at the time you said and banged on your window. Tap, tap, tap, I heard – that morning, on the bottom right-hand window pane. The other panes were missing and patched with cardboard. I was in the big bed with my brothers, Peter and James. We were lying like spoons, three in a row. My two big sisters were snoring in their bed on the other side of the room.

I opened my eyes. My first thought, as always, was – has James wet the bed? He was only four years old and when he woke in the night he was too frightened to go and sit on the chamber-pot by himself. Sometimes he would wake me and ask me to take him. But sometimes he would just do it in the bed. I stretched my arm over Peter and felt under James. No, the mattress was dry. You see, we didn't have a sheet. We'd only the one and the girls got that.

Tap, tap, tap, I heard again, and then I heard Pat Sweeney's low voice in the alley below, 'Hey, Archie O'Hanlon, get up and show your face. I haven't got all night to stand around waiting for you to get up.'

I hopped out of bed. The floorboards were gritty and cold. I shivered. We had a bit of old sack which hung down over the window for a curtain. I lifted it up. I saw the vague outline of Pat Sweeney in the darkness. He had a candle in a lantern without which he would never have found his way round the maze of alleys where we lived on the Dublin north side.

I banged on the pane of glass. Sweeney waved the candle and called, 'Morning, Archie. Another lovely day.' Whatever the weather, that's what he always said.

Pat 'Knocker' Sweeney was an old soldier. He was shot in the leg in Afghanistan. When the bullet was taken out something didn't go right. Now I could hear him limping away.

I groped my way out of the room and on to the landing. We five children had the big front room. My parents had the other, smaller room, the one at the back. I could hear my father wheezing and breathing.

I went downstairs. At the bottom was what we called

the kitchen. We didn't have a parlour. There was also a scullery at the back, more a cupboard than a room really, with a hand pump and a sink that emptied straight into the back yard.

Red coals glowed in the grate under a coat of powdery slack that mother put on last thing the night before to keep the fire in. I gave the fire a riddle. The ash dropped down and the embers flared up. I put on a shovel's worth of good coal. The kettle was on the table. My mother always left it ready and filled with water. It held enough to half fill the tin bath. Once I could barely lift it to hang it on the crane. But now, after six months in the dining-car, I was stronger. It dropped on to the hook. I swung the crane round and got the kettle over the embers.

Now came what I dreaded. I couldn't hold on until I could use the lavatory at Broadstone Station, nor could I go back upstairs and use the chamber pot. I had a job now. I had to act like a man.

I put my father's slippers on, lit a candle in the fire and went out into the yard. It was so icy cold it hurt my lungs to breathe. The privy was in the corner. The door was closed. With the sweeping brush, I gave the door a bang and then another bang. If there was a rat inside, this would drive him out. I waited, holding my candle over the holes along the bottom of the privy door so that if anything ran out, I would see it. But nothing did. I hit the door again for safety. Then, holding the candle in front of me and peering ahead, I went inside.

Our privy was a seat with a hole above a dry toilet. Every month a man came and emptied the toilet for sixpence. If we didn't have a sixpence then my father did it. It was near the end of the month so the privy was full. I held the candle over the hole and looked down.

Sometimes a rat would fall in and be swimming around in the mess. You had to watch out for that. They could jump up and give you a nasty bite you-know-where.

But I saw nothing moving in the muck. The smell was awful, of course. I did what I had to do. My mother got old roses from the market and stewed the leaves for hours to make the rosewater in the bucket in the corner: she said it kept down the smell in the privy. I didn't think it made the slightest bit of difference but I poured a little down, then I went back out into the yard. I took the milk jug from the window ledge where we kept it on cold nights to stop our milk souring.

The water in the kettle wasn't boiling. I put a splash in the ewer, took off my vest, and washed my face and hands and ears at the kitchen table. I could feel the hairs growing under my nose and on my chin. I would have to shave one day soon, my father said. I cleaned the black bits from under my nails with a pointed stick my father had whittled for me. If my hands weren't clean, Mr Cribben would send me home. He always said, 'If you're filthy, then the customers won't eat the food.'

My clothes were on the rack over the fire. I wore straight leg trousers with a stripe down the side (same colour as the company livery) and a reefer jacket. It was double-breasted with nice buttons and epaulettes and the company initials MGWR on the cuffs. My boots were black. My mother had polished them the night before. They stood in the corner on an old page from the *Freeman's Journal*. I also had gloves and a hat, but these stayed in my cubicle in the galley beside the dining-room with my apron. Mr Cribben wouldn't let me take these home in case I lost them.

By the time I had dressed, the kettle had boiled. I levered the top off the caddy and put four spoonfuls of tea into the pot. When I put in the hot water the lovely smell of tea rose up. When I smell tea now, it puts me straight back then. Other smells, say, the smell of yeast that came from the brewery across the river, the smell of rotting leaves in the Phoenix Park, the wet of Dublin pavements after rain, the smell of the sweat of horses, none of these bring back those long gone winter mornings as much as the simple smell of tea.

I ran up the stairs and went to the door of the back bedroom.

'It's time to get up,' I called inside.

'I'll be down,' my mother whispered.

I went to the kitchen and cut a piece of bread. I stabbed it with a fork and held it over the fire. My mother came down in an old army greatcoat over her night-dress. She poured the tea; one for her, one for me.

'You're a good boy,' she said.

She said this because I gave her my earnings every Saturday night when I came home.

I ate my toast dry and drank my tea; then I kissed her and left the house.

Outside, I found it was one of those winter mornings when the wet seems to be everywhere although it isn't raining, and it's so cold you'd think everything should be frozen by rights but it isn't. The dirt of the ground was dark grey. The puddles were shiny and black. I was careful not to dirty my boots because as Mr Cribben said, 'If you're filthy, then the customers won't eat the food.'

At the end of the alley I turned into the street. There were gas lamps here, white light that lit up the bottom of the lamppost, but that got weaker as it went out into the darkness.

I hurried on. Paving-stones made the going easier. I heard my boots, and the clip-clop of a horse, and the grumble of cart wheels on cobblestones. I could also hear the hissing of the lamps. Sometimes I'd think Dublin was really a giant and the noise of the gas lamps was really him breathing.

When I got to Broadstone I went straight to the clock, as I always did. It was big, with a white face with black numbers, and a gas lamp with a reflector close to it. There was enough light to read the time. It was just before five a.m. I started at five. Mr Cribben was also fussy about timekeeping.

I went into the station proper. I passed a porter pushing a dogcart piled with mailbags.

'Morning, Archie,' he called.

There were trains hissing, porters moving around with carts loaded with milk churns. I heard a whistle blow and a train start to shunt away. The day had started the same as every other day started except this would be one I would never, ever, forget.

I found my train at platform eight. I was on the Dublin to Achill Island run that day. The 'Down' train, what was called the Limited Mail, left at seven-thirty, arriving Achill just after two o'clock. The 'Up' train left Achill at three-thirty and was back in Broadstone by ten o'clock. I did one day on and one day off and every other week I did a Sunday.

Mr Cribben was standing on the platform beside the dining car. He was already in his chef's clothes; a white coat and a big white puffy hat. He was a very big man. He weighed eighteen or twenty stone.

'You're just in time,' he said.

His eyes were funny. One of them was looking at me but the other one was looking somewhere else. Some called him Lazy Eye behind his back but they wouldn't have dared to his face. Mr Cribben didn't have a sense of humour. He did have a terrible temper.

'Hello, Mr Cribben,' I said politely.

I did not want to be on Mr Cribben's bad side. And I never was, I think; Mr Cribben could be rough, he could be rude, he could say terrible things, but he never hit me, and he made certain I ate properly. In time, when I got used to him, I saw there was much to like, or at least admire. Mr Cribben was painfully honest. He never took food home like some of the other railway cooks. He never took coal home, either. If a passenger left something valuable in the dining-car (and they did all the time, you wouldn't believe what passengers left behind) he never kept it but always returned it to lost property. He hated dishonesty. He hated it with a passion. It was his influence that made me become a policeman later, but that's another story.

'Right, let's have a look at you,' he said.

He pulled me down the platform and stood me under the hissing gas lamp.

'Nails,' he said.

I lifted my hands up. I can't imagine he could see anything in that light but he looked at them carefully anyway.

'Right,' he said, apparently satisfied, 'ears.'

I dropped my head forward. Mr Cribben looked first behind each ear and then at my neck.

'Boots,' he said.

I turned round and then lifted first one boot and then the other. He was looking for muck on the soles. It was so easy, in the dark, to step in horse's muck or worse and then tramp it into the train. If my boots were dirty I'd have to go out to the front of the station and clean them on the boot-scraper by the entrance. But they were clean.

'Right,' said Mr Cribben, 'spuds, me boy.'

I climbed into the train and went into the small galley.

The oven was already on. Mr Cribben came in at four to fire it up. I hung my jacket up and put on an apron. There was ten stone of potatoes on the floor in a sack. I dragged them on to the platform; I went back and got the slop bucket for the peel, a bowl of water, and a paring knife and a box. For the next hour and a half, sitting on the platform, I peeled spuds for the three meals – breakfast, lunch and dinner. And Mr Cribben made the soup and steamed the puddings and put the kedgeree on to cook. There was a strong smell of fish.

When I finished peeling, my hands were sore. My skin felt gritty. Mr Cribben fried me two rashers and an egg. I ate them straight out of the pan; I used a piece of bread instead of a fork.

'One thing less to wash,' Mr Cribben said.

I had to wipe and polish all the cutlery and lay up the tables in the dining-car. Through the window I saw a train pull up at the platform opposite and passengers stream out. They had come in from the suburbs and had to be in their offices by eight. I always enjoyed that time of day and I liked banging the heavy knives and forks down on the starched tablecloths and knowing that I had been hard at work long before most people were even awake.

When I finished laying up, I took off my apron and put my good jacket back on; I put on my hat and gloves. Now I was ready.

I went and stood on the platform and enjoyed watching passengers file past and climb aboard. In the same way, I know actors like to look out from the wings and see their audience as they come in and sit down.

It could be profitable too. Sometimes, when I was serving a passenger in the dining-car who remembered seeing me, it was always that bit easier to start talking. I would tell them what time I had started and that would make them feel sorry for me and give me a bigger than usual tip. It all helped. My father couldn't work, for he was sick in his chest. The doctor called it catarrh. He had a horrible hacking cough and he wheezed and he could barely walk for lack of air. My mother took in laundry and my sisters cleaned houses in Howth. None of them brought in much. I was the only one with a real job and I had to bring home as much as possible.

A man was approaching. He seemed to be as wide as he was high, with short legs and tiny feet. I think I first noticed him because he took these small little steps, yet for all that he moved very quickly down the platform. He was wearing a black and bright yellow tweed jacket with matching knickerbockers, a peaked hat, yellow woollen socks and gaiters. Sportsmen in tweed, going west to fish or shoot, were common on the train; however, none I had ever seen made me think, as this man did, of a wasp.

'What are you looking at?' asked the man, when he drew closer. I felt my face go red.

'Is the breakfast any good today, or is it the swill they usually serve?'

'It'll be very good, sir,' I said.

'Really.' He sniffed the air.

'It's kedgeree, sir,' I said. 'It's really very good.'

'But if it was awful, do you think you'd tell me?'

'There's other things to eat, too.'

'That's a lame reply, if ever there was one. Answer the question. If you were serving tripe would you tell me? No, of course you wouldn't. In which case, kindly keep your opinions on your fare to yourself. Now, I want a table,' he barked.

'Just one, is it, sir?' I said, pulling from my pocket a notebook and pencil.

'Do you see anyone with me? No, I don't think so. Yes, I am only one but I want a whole table.'

'You can't have a whole table. If you had a whole table that would be three places that couldn't be used by anyone else . . .'

'What's wrong with that?' he interrupted.

'We put people together. I will put you here, table one.' I gestured at table one through the glass. 'You may be sharing. The views of the Hill of Down and northwards towards Navan are marvellous.'

'Oh, are they?' he replied sarcastically.

He stared closely at me. His face was round and smooth; the skin glowed with health; his eyes were liquorice black.

'Are you stupid?' he continued.

I was completely at a loss.

I opened my mouth and I closed my mouth. 'I don't understand,' I said, at last.

'I said, are you stupid? Simple question. Even a moron should be able to manage it. Thick or not thick, which are you, little boy?'

At that moment Mr Cribben put his head out the doorway. He must have heard the man's voice.

'Can I help you, sir?' he said.

'Maybe you can,' said the stranger. 'Is this boy stupid? He doesn't appear to be able to answer this remarkably straightforward question.'

'No,' said Mr Cribben, without batting an eyelid, 'he's not stupid. Why do you need to know?'

'Because I can't stand stupid people. They're insufferable. And when as I intend, I take breakfast, providing it isn't disgusting, I insist, at the very least, that the boy who waits on my table is highly intelligent.'

'Are you travelling first class?' asked Mr Cribben coldly.

'Yes,' said the man, slowly.

'First class is up here,' I said, pointing, 'one carriage up.'

'Ah,' said the stranger, 'you are intelligent after all.' He looked me up and down, coolly; then he stared at my right ear, and after that my left ear.

'Do you know what?' he said, finally.

'No, sir,' Mr Cribben replied. He was still polite but cold.

'He's actually clean behind his ears. Can I commend you on that.'

'Oh.' Mr Cribben smiled, thawing a little. 'Yes. I always insist.'

'Now,' the stranger continued, turning to me, 'I want a

seat at that table you suggested, and I want to sit facing the engine.'

'Back to the engine's more comfortable and the view's better . . .'

'Don't you listen?' he said, fiercely. 'I want to face the engine. My name is Cink, with a C, Mister, initials D, L, O, got it?'

'C – I – N – K,' I said, spelling the name out as I scribbled it in my book.

'Oh,' he said, turning back to me, 'when the man comes with my luggage, send him on down to me.'

'How will I know your luggage?'

'Oh, you'll know,' said Mr Cink, and he spun off.

'What an extraordinarily unpleasant fellow that Mr Cink is,' said Mr Cribben, before he disappeared into the galley again.

A few moments later a porter came past. He pushed a handcart piled high with leather suitcases, fishing rods, gun cases, shooting sticks, hat boxes, and various sporting items. Every piece of luggage had a yellow ribbon tied on, and it all looked new and expensive.

'Mr Cink, he's in the first first-class carriage,' I said, pointing the way to the porter.

The porter trudged on. One of the handcart wheels clicked and groaned. It needed oiling. After the handcart had passed on I noticed a faint sulphur smell, like bad eggs, hanging in the air.

* * *

15

The guard blew his whistle. He dropped his flag. I felt the floor of the galley juddering.

The carriage swayed and creaked. I went out to the corridor and looked through a window. There was a man waving his cloth cap at someone in the train. The train began to move slowly past him. Gradually the train got faster and faster. We came out from under the canopy into rain. As we pulled further from the station, I saw gleaming silver rails beneath me, one beside the other, like neat lines on paper. I saw greasy sleepers and between the sleepers, the black and white pebbles on which the railway rested. I saw houses with crooked windows. I saw roofs, the tiles wet and gleaming. I saw tiny little yards crowded with stables and sheds. I saw a huge cloud of steam and smoke filled with spots of black soot billowing past. The whistle sounded, sharp and thrilling. We'd started. We were on our way. I always loved this moment.

'Come on boy, stop dreaming,' said Mr Cribben, putting his head out of the galley door. 'Get the tea ready, will you. Look sharp.'

'Yes, Mr Cribben.'

I made the tea in a huge pot and left it on the side of the stove to stew. Mr Cribben stood over a huge vat of rice and fish which he turned with a long-handled spoon.

'Every man has his price,' he said, 'and mine is mighty small.'

Mr Cribben said this all the time when he was working. It wasn't that he didn't like the job. It was just that his work was hard. He started early; he finished late. He had a sick child at home, a boy with bad lungs. His wife suffered with the nerves. They had had a daughter but she had been killed by a runaway horse on Baggot Street bridge.

I left the galley and set off along the train. The first-class carriages had a corridor down the side with compartments leading off it.

'Breakfast! Breakfast is served, ladies and gentlemen,' I called.

There were very few people on board. Some of the compartments were empty. It occurred to me that only a few passengers had trickled by when I was on the platform. It was unusual. There were always large numbers of people going west, sportsmen especially. Perhaps the winter was too cold, too severe, and this had put everyone off, although the truth was I had no idea.

I opened a door to the tenth compartment. I saw three men. Mr Cink was in the far corner with his back to the guard's van. He had his hat on his finger and he was turning it round and round. The racks above, on both sides, were crammed with Mr Cink's luggage.

'Oh, it's Hermes,' he said.

I knew exactly who Hermes was. I had done all the Greek gods at Connor Street National School.

'And what do you want?' continued Mr Cink.

'Breakfast is served.'

'Is it? What is it?'

'We've kedgeree.'

'So you said earlier . . . very exotic.' Mr Cink turned to face the two men on the seat opposite. 'We've only just become acquainted but would you care to join me at breakfast? We can continue our fascinating discussion over a plate of kedgeree.' He swivelled his head towards me.

'The salmon is fresh?'

'Yes, sir, fresh from the market this very morning.'

'That sounds very pleasant.'

'I'm glad you think so, Mr Fee,' said Mr Cink, politely, but he managed to sound rude too.

Mr Fee had white hair and a square head and a small round body. He wore a bowler hat and a black coat.

'And what about you Mr Smyth?' Mr Cink continued.

The other man had very short hair and a strange stare. It was only later that I realised he hardly blinked.

'All right,' said Mr Smyth.

'Do you like stories, young man?' Mr Cink barked as I turned to go.

'Yes,' I said.

'What kind?'

How did one answer a question like this? I liked *Aesop's Fables*. I liked Lamb's *Tales from Shakespeare*. I liked *The Children of Lir*. I had read Charles Dickens' *A Tale of Two Cities* and *Oliver Twist*. There were lots of other stories I liked, as well. But listing my likes would get on Mr Cink's nerves, I guessed. I decided on a simple, general answer.

'I like any kind, sir,' I said.

'So! You don't discriminate,' said Mr Cink, quite nastily.

'You'll read any one at all will you, any story at all, and whatever the story is, you'll be happy with it?'

'No,' I said. 'Obviously I don't like all stories the same. I like some more than others.'

'Yes, yes, yes,' said Mr Cink. 'I'm bored with this line of conversation. Learn to stick your head above the parapet, child, and have opinions.'

'Do you prefer to hear it, or do you prefer to read it yourself, a story that is?' asked Mr Smyth, the man with the strange intense stare. I had loved it when Mr Rowley, our schoolmaster, had read to us but I knew it would seem childish if I said so.

'I prefer to read a story to myself,' I said. I thought that sounded grown-up. 'But I can listen quietly if required.' I thought that also sounded nicely grown-up.

'So, you can read, can you?' said Mr Cink.

'Oh, yes,' I said, quietly.

'Well! The schools must be doing something right nowadays, if cook's boy on the Midland Great Western Railway of Ireland knows his letters,' Mr Cink said next in a booming voice.

Now I realised why Mr Cink had asked if I could read. It was for the sake of his quip that followed.

Mr Fee took off his bowler and began to run his finger round the rim. He laughed quietly.

'As a society we really are making progress, you know,' said Mr Fee, 'slowly but surely. A hundred years ago, we'd be making this journey by coach and horses. Achill would be, I don't know, a week away from the capital. No railway then. Today, thanks to this,' he pointed at the floor, 'we'll be there by this afternoon. In the year of our Lord, eighteen hundred and ninety-nine, you can get from the east coast of Ireland to the west coast of Ireland in about seven hours; that's staggering progress. And, what's more, the majority of our children now go to school. That's progress too.'

'Yes, yes, yes,' Mr Cink interrupted impatiently, 'Marvellous! Seven hours better than seven days but that's still seven hours we have to kill. Now, we can eat, we can doze, we can smoke our pipes *but* none of these are a good use of our time, are they? No! We need something to sharpen us up, something to keep us on our toes.'

'Good morning, gentlemen,' I broke in. I stepped back and slid the door closed behind me.

A few minutes later, I was back in my place in the dining-room. I had gone to every first-class compartment. I had told the handful of first-class passengers that breakfast was being served. But so far, no one had come. It was very odd. I felt nervous.

I was bored, so I looked out the window.

Mr Fee appeared at the other end of the dining-car. Mr Smyth and Mr Cink followed behind.

'Oh,' Mr Cink shouted towards me, 'I see you're busy.' He laughed.

I put the three men at number one, the table closest to the galley.

'Porridge?'

The three men nodded. I went into the galley, got three bowls of porridge and went back to the table.

'Do you think grown men should enjoy stories?' Mr Cink asked.

I thought about this for a moment. 'My father likes Charles Dickens,' I said. 'He read him when he was at sea.'

'Oh, a bookish clan, are we?'

I said nothing.

'What's your name?'

Mr Smyth's big square face with its big blue eyes was pointing in my direction.

'Archie,' I said.

'Oh, an Archibald,' Mr Cink exclaimed and laughed. He clapped his hands. 'We're being waited on by an Archibald. It's too good to be true.'

My face went red. I did not like my full name. I was named after my mother's father. He was a grocer who owned a shop in Navan. My mother idolised him. He died of cholera in Dundalk.

'Don't pay any attention to him,' Mr Smyth continued, nodding in the direction of Mr Cink, in case I didn't understand who he was talking about. 'Archie what?' he said.

'O'Hanlon.'

'O'Hanlon,' said Mr Fee. 'I taught several boys called O'Hanlon.'

'Where is everybody, Archie?' Mr Cink asked, salting

his porridge. 'It's like a morgue in here.'

'I don't know,' I said.

'I'm not complaining. I like an empty dining-car,' Mr Smyth said slowly. He swirled a piece of butter around the middle of his porridge. 'I don't like it when people are gathered together. Their talking disturbs me.'

'Ah, a misanthropist,' said Mr Cink. 'That's a hater of mankind, Archie, in case you don't know.'

'Just because you don't like chatter, doesn't mean you don't like mankind,' said Mr Smyth sharply. The butter knob had melted. A thin yellow watery sheen of grease spread over his porridge.

'Give me silence. Save me from the nonsense people talk, especially when they're travelling, and I am a happy man. Inflict noise and banter on me and I become a brute.' Mr Smyth slipped a spoon of porridge into his mouth.

'For what we are about to receive,' Mr Fee said quietly. He made a rapid sign of the cross.

'Sorry,' said Mr Smyth, though his mouth was full. He dropped his spoon with a clatter. 'I didn't realise you were saying grace.' Mr Cink said nothing. He just glanced across at Mr Fee briefly, an expression of disdain on his face, then began to eat.

I went and stood in my place against the wall again. The three men began to talk about stories: Irish stories and stories from the rest of the world.

The men finished their porridge but not their talk. They were so absorbed they did not even move back in their seats to make it easier for me to reach their plates. I heard Mr Fee saying, 'A great story, badly told, will carry an audience, whereas a bad story, no matter how brilliantly it's told, never, ever will.'

'Will you gentlemen all be taking the kedgeree?' I asked.

The men nodded assent and went on talking. I slipped off.

'Is it really just three in?' Mr Cribben asked, as I came through the door into the galley.

'Yes,' I said and put the plates down.

'Where is everyone?' Mr Cribben wondered. 'I've never known the train to be so empty. Look at it. At this rate, we'll have to do kedgeree for lunch and dinner and breakfast tomorrow again.'

He made up three plates of kedgeree.

'I hope they like it and show their appreciation by leaving a very lavish tip.'

I went back to the table with the plates of food. The men were leaning forward on their elbows. Talk had turned to argument.

'I believe,' said Mr Cink, 'that I have a story to tell and that I will tell it better than you, Mr Fee, had you a story to tell, or than you, Mr Smyth.'

'Gentlemen,' I said, interrupting the conversation.

'Ah Hermes, bringer of dinner. Or breakfast,' Mr Cink corrected himself.

I put the plates down, then went and stood in my place again.

'You're talking nonsense,' said Mr Smyth.

'I agree,' said Mr Fee. 'You're making an assertion that can't be supported. There's no way to prove it.'

'Oh, but there is,' said Mr Cink. He sprinkled pepper over his rice. It looked like spots of soot on snow. 'You have a judge and as you said yourself, earlier, quality will always shine through. Any judge will recognise it. The best story will always outshine its rivals.'

Mr Fee pondered this. Mr Smyth was silent. Mr Cink began to eat quickly. The kedgeree was very hot and each time a forkful went on his tongue, I would hear him breathing out quickly to cool it down. He didn't stop talking though.

'I tell you what. I formally challenge you to a duel of words. I will pit myself, my story, my storytelling, against yours.'

The three of them now wrangled about this storytelling competition. Most of what was said was above my head except for Mr Cink's repeated boasts that he was the supreme teller of tales among the three of them.

'But I am better than *you*, I know I am,' Mr Smyth countered.

'No, you're not.'

'Yes, I am, and I bet Mr Fee is better than you as well.'

'Does this mean you are formally accepting my challenge?' asked Mr Cink. He sounded joyful.

'Yes, I am,' said Mr Smyth. 'I am accepting your challenge.'

'You can leave me out of this,' said Mr Fee.

'No, I cannot,' said Mr Cink. 'A challenge has been issued. It cannot now be withdrawn.'

'I said count me out,' Mr Fee said quietly. 'We've far too many competitions in Ireland. We're always judging best dancer, best fiddler. It's fine for the winners, but awful for the losers, as we schoolmasters know. I'll tell you a story but I won't have it judged. I concede, even before we begin, that you Mr Cink, and you Mr Smyth, will tell a better tale than I.'

'If it's between you and I,' said Mr Smyth, turning to Mr Cink, 'Mr Fee could be the judge, couldn't he?'

'Don't be ridiculous,' said Mr Cink. 'He'll pick you. You don't want to win because you had an unfair advantage? Of course you don't. You're miles too honest. I've a better idea.' He pointed at me. 'Come here,' he said.

'Me?'

'Do you see anyone else? Of course you. And don't you know it's rude to say "Me?" like that?'

I said nothing.

'Right, don't look so surprised, Archie, we've got a little job for you.'

I had a good idea what this was. I also had a good idea I didn't want it.

'We're each going to tell a story – isn't that what we've agreed, gentlemen? – and you will then judge which is the best one.'

'Except I'm not in the competition,' said Mr Fee.

'Yes, he's being boring,' Mr Cink said. 'So, Archie,

follow us to our compartment. You've work to do, boy.'

'I can't. I'm at work and I have to clear up when you go.'

'You can't. I'm sorry, I don't know the meaning of this word, can't.'

'I'm at work. I have to clear up when you go.'

'Oh come off it,' said Mr Cink staring around. 'Be a good lad and leave clearing till later. All you've got to do is listen to three stories. It won't take long.'

'Sir, I can't leave.'

Mr Cink pulled out his wallet, fished out a note and dropped it on the table.

'I see. Then I have to get permission to take you away for a few hours. All right.'

He hurtled towards the galley.

'Passengers aren't allowed in there,' I called.

'I am,' Mr Cink said bluntly. 'By the way, don't follow me in.'

After a few minutes Mr Cink returned.

'There's no obstacle on earth too big for Mr Cink.' He looked at me. He rubbed his hands. 'Right, gentlemen, shall we go back to the compartment and commence the Battle Royal?'

'I'm not in the competition,' Mr Fee said quietly but firmly.

'I know, you're the warm-up,' Mr Cink said, 'before the main attraction.' He smiled, turned away and strode between the tables towards the far door.

Mr Smyth, still seated, shook his head while he drew

his wallet from his pocket. 'I've never met anyone quite like him,' he murmured to Mr Fee. 'Have you?'

'Archie,' Mr Cink called back over his shoulder. 'Take for all the breakfasts from the note on the table and bring the rest of the change down to my compartment. And Archie, buck up. You've got three stories to hear before Achill.'

'Oh,' said the two other gentleman, standing and following Mr Cink towards the end of the carriage. 'Oh, thank you for that breakfast, Mr Cink, that was most generous . . .'

I took the bank note from the table. It was a white Bank of England note, value £10. No tip had been mentioned, alas. Oh well, it wasn't worth thinking about these things.

I went into the galley. Mr Cribben stood at the stove.

'Archie,' he said, smiling. 'Look here.'

He held a bright shining sovereign between finger and thumb. There was a picture of old Queen Victoria in her widow's weeds on it.

'The queer fellow in the yellow tweed,' he said, 'he bunged me a sovereign to let you away for a while. All you've got to do is listen to him and the other fellows telling a story, then choose the best one. For ten-and-six – your half of this – that sounds like pretty easy work, my lad.'

'But shouldn't I be here with you?' I said this really for form's sake. Mr Cribben shook his head.

Ten-and-six, I thought, opening the money drawer and throwing in Mr Cink's note. Never in my life had I ever had such a large tip. Oh yes, for this, I'd listen happily to their stories but I wouldn't pick Mr Cink as the winner just because he gave me the tip. No, I'd pick what I thought was the best story, who ever told it. Fourteen I might be, but I knew the difference between right and wrong. I wasn't for sale.

I began to count out Mr Cink's change.

'I'll put this in our jar,' said Mr Cribben. I heard the clink as the sovereign landed on the other coins inside, all of them coppers with a threepence or two thrown in. We never got silver or gold tips. 'I don't know how you did it, Archie,' Mr Cribben continued, 'but you've impressed that fellow in yellow. And I'm impressed too. Ten-and-six.'

I smiled and nodded. I was about to get what it took me a month to earn.

'Will you call me back if passengers start coming?' I asked.

'For ten-and-six, Archie, I can manage a full sitting on my own, thank you very much.'

'All right,' I said. I put Mr Cink's change in my pocket, then pulled off my apron and hung it by the door.

'Good judging,' Mr Cribben called from behind as I left the galley.

'Thank you,' I shouted back. I was in high spirits.

Part Two

Soul Cages

Mr Cink sat by the window; I gave him his change. I sat down at the other end of the seat from him. Mr Smyth sat opposite Mr Cink and Mr Fee was in the corner opposite me.

'This story is called "Soul Cages,"' said Mr Fee gently.

'Oh, good,' said Mr Cink, sounding as if he meant exactly the opposite. 'All about good and evil, is it?'

'Don't try to undermine me,' said Mr Fee. 'It won't make you any better when your turn comes.' Mr Fee winked at me. 'And the young man here won't like you any the more for it, either.'

'You're not in the competition so quit complaining,' said Mr Cink.

'As you wish,' said Mr Fee. 'Treat me as the overture the orchestra plays before the curtain goes up. I don't count.' He seemed weary suddenly.

'My story is going to be so brilliant,' said Mr Cink, 'you're going to be thankful you're not in. You've saved yourself from public humiliation.'

Mr Fee looked at me and rolled his eyes. 'I shall begin. Please do not interrupt . . .'

' There was once a man called Micky Mealiffe, who lived on the coast of County Mayo. His father and grandfather were fishermen before him. He lived alone with his wife, Peggy.

It was often wondered why three generations of Mealiffes chose to live in a place which was one, accessible only by a narrow twisting mountain road, and two, seven miles from the nearest neighbour.

The answer was simple: in front of the cabin – but hidden behind a screen of pine trees planted by cunning grandfather Mealiffe – there lay a creek. It was a nice snug one, where a boat might sit out a storm, warm and safe as a fox in his lair.

And at the end of the creek, where the land gave way to the water, a ledge of sunken rock stuck out some half a mile into the sea.

Imagine something like a wall, about a dozen feet wide, lying about the height of a man below the surface. This wall marched out in a straight line along the sea-bed, and the drop on either side to the ocean floor was several hundred feet.

Imagine then, one dark winter's night, a ship approaching this spot; like many ships before her, she was blown ashore by a terrible storm raging out in the Atlantic.

"I want a man at the front taking soundings every few seconds," the Captain ordered.

The bo'sun selected a mariner and he went forward, dropped a plumb into the ocean and let the line pay out after it as the plumb sunk down through the foaming brine . . .

The Captain's prudence was right in principle but it wouldn't do him any good in the end, would it? Because with the wall sticking up, as it did, from the sea floor, the plumb wouldn't strike it until it was too late, and the ship was about to hit the rock and smash to smithereens.

Suddenly, there was an almighty wrench as the wooden keel of the vessel was torn asunder. The boat began to sink, fast.

"Light the distress rockets," the Captain ordered.

The rockets were lit and, one after another, they whooshed up into the sky.

"Hey, Micky, look, over there," said Mrs Mealiffe, who at that moment was tipping used tea leaves just outside the front door.

"What did you say, Peggy?" asked Micky. He went to the door, looked up, and he saw the stream of yellow and red light made by the distress rocket in the dismal stormy sky.

"There's a ship sinking," said Mrs Mealiffe, smiling.

Micky ran down to the creek, got aboard his coracle and cast off.

He paddled along the creek and out on to the open sea.

He saw nothing and he heard nothing except for the crashing of the waves on the rocks behind.

Micky had done his duty. He was about to turn round and paddle home when he thought he heard human cries. "Hello," Micky shouted.

"Hello," a voice shouted back from the darkness.

"Swim towards my light," shouted Micky. He lifted the lantern from the stern and waved it in the air.

He heard laboured breathing and the splash of someone swimming through the sea.

Micky scanned the water. He saw a wet head. At first he thought it was a seal but then Micky heard the cry, "Help me!"

In quick order, Micky dragged the man out of the water and into his coracle. It was the sailor who'd stood at the front of the vessel taking soundings.

Micky paddled frantically back to the creek, tied up and carried the cold, shivering, water-logged mariner up the path and into his tidy warm little cabin.

Peggy was waiting. She had prepared hot poítin, the illegally-made alcohol that was clear like water. She wrapped the mariner in a blanket, held the glass to his lips and said, "Drink."

In the morning the mariner awoke.

"Where am I?" he asked, sleepily.

"In the house of Micky Mealiffe and his wife, Peggy," Micky replied.

"How did I come here?"

"Your ship sunk."

"Oh yes, my ship," he said, groggy from sleep and drink. "We were going so well, and then suddenly there was a terrible bang and next thing I was in the sea. What was that she hit?"

The mariners that Micky saved (and he had saved several over the years, for Micky, it must be emphasised, was a tender-hearted fellow) always asked him this question, and Micky always gave them the same answer.

"I don't know," said Micky carefully. "I never go more than a few yards from the shore, and I haven't a notion what's out where I imagine you must have been."

This was a lie. Micky loved nothing better, on calm days, than to sail out in his coracle and gaze down at the wall that had sunk so many ships. Like his father and grandfather before him, Micky always imagined that the wide line of rock that he saw running below the surface of the sea was once a road that led to a castle, Castle Mealiffe of course, the ancestral home, that had long since been swallowed by the sea.

"So you wouldn't know," persisted the mariner, "what we hit?"

"Haven't a notion," said Micky, "but what I do know is you're hungry – aren't I right?"

"Oh yes," agreed the mariner, again not knowing that this was what Micky always said.

Peggy fried bacon and potatoes and made strong brown

tea. When the food was finished, Micky offered a pipe. The two men puffed away for half an hour. The room slowly filled with blue-black smoke.

Having finished his smoke, Micky bent forward and whispered to the mariner, "Come outside for a moment, will you?" Then he glanced in the direction of Peggy, who was knitting in the corner, and raised his eyes heavenwards.

"Of course," said the mariner, quick to understand that his host had something to tell him alone.

Micky and his guest hurried out of the crooked front door and into the little garden. Immediately in front of the cabin stood a line of pine trees. These screened the creek and the sea below.

"A windbreak," Micky explained quickly, and he led the mariner round to the back of his cabin, to the start of the road that led to the outside world.

"Here," Micky said quickly, and before the mariner could say or do anything, Micky put two new shining guineas into the palm of the mariner's hand.

"What's this for?" asked the mariner, surprised but not displeased.

"I don't want you to go begging your way home," said Micky.

It was a phrase that left no room for doubt. It was time to go, the mariner realised.

Now two guineas is a nice tidy sum. There is no man in the world who wouldn't want two guineas if they were pressed in his hand. But there also is no man in the world, either, who wants to appear eager in a situation like this.

There was a silence as the mariner collected his thoughts.

Micky pressed on. "Don't worry," he said. "You can drop me back the money when you next sail past."

"I could," said the mariner, "and indeed, I will."

Meanwhile, the mariner thought to himself, I've got two guineas in my hand which are mine to keep. I'll just say goodbye and never return to this godforsaken place ever again.

"You've been kindness itself, sir, and I will now say goodbye," said the mariner. He shook hands with Micky and he set off up the track.

Micky watched until the mariner had disappeared from sight. Then he sat on a rock and smoked his second pipe of the day. He wanted to be certain the man wasn't coming back. He enjoyed the idea of what he had purchased for so ludicrous and so small an outlay.

Micky circled his cabin, then followed the path through the screen of pine trees. The creek stretching in front of him was full of bobbing wooden boxes, lengths of rope and bits of wood.

This was what Micky was so anxious that no mariner saw. When a ship foundered on the long rock, its contents, instead of scattering along the coast, always washed up in his creek as a piece. Always. It was something to do with the rock, the shape of the creek and the tides.

"Well, Micky," said Peggy, appearing noiselessly, "what's the estate produced this morning?"

Micky took a gaff from a shed, used it to snag one of the bobbing boxes and dragged it ashore. When he got the box on the beach he saw what it was.

"Tea," he said. "It's tea, today."

"You should get a good price for all that tea," said Peggy. She liked money, as she freely admitted. Micky was intimate with several shop keepers who paid him good money and never asked questions.

"Aye," said Micky.

Micky now looked sad. "This creek wouldn't be full only a ship's gone down and her crew with her."

"Now, Micky, give over, no sadness, you know sadness does you no good," said Peggy.

"So many lives lost, so many women bereaved, so many children left without a father," Micky continued. (He rather enjoyed the way this sentence rolled as he spoke it.)

Peggy never liked such talk. "Micky, did you sink the ship? Did you lure her to her doom with false beacons? Of course you didn't. The ship sunk – like all the ships sink out there – when she hit a rock in a storm that was not of your making.

"Now then Micky Mealiffe, you have to ask yourself, did you do your best? And what's the answer? Yes, you did. You did do your best. You got in your coracle, you sailed out to sea, and you saved a life, didn't you?

"So who could blame you now, Micky? You're just picking up what's left, rather than see it go to waste. We'd all do the same if we were in your shoes, even that mariner to whom you said goodbye this morning."

As usual, Peggy's good sense banished Micky's prickles of conscience.

"Yes, there's no point in dwelling on what's over and done with," he agreed. "Just concentrate on the business in hand . . ." ”

'I agree entirely,' said Mr Cink, interrupting the storyteller.

Mr Fee ignored him and continued . . .

‘ So, having quelled his conscience, and whistling brightly to himself, Micky reached with the gaff for a second box of tea and began to drag it ashore.

"I'm up home, so," said Peggy. "I'll hitch the donkey to the cart and bring her down."

Peggy padded up the path in her bare feet. She wore a long black work-dress and a starched white apron. Her head was bare.

When she got to the line of pine trees Peggy stopped and looked back. Micky had already dragged half a dozen boxes ashore. She liked to watch him at this work.

She had met Micky when he came to her father's pub in Ballina to sell casks of beer that had also washed into his creek. She was a pretty girl of eighteen. Micky had asked her to marry him almost at once. He was charming, talkative and funny and he sang beautifully, but Peggy said no. Undeterred, Micky kept coming back and she kept saying no. She was a level-headed girl; although she saw the point of charm, she knew that wealth was what ultimately determined a successful marriage.

Peggy's continuous refusals baffled Micky until the future father-in-law took him aside and explained she was waiting for some proof of his ability to support her.

So Micky let Peggy into his secret. "I'll marry you," she said, and they had married and moved to this little cabin. She had lived so comfortably and so happily here, these last five years, that there hadn't once been a single moment when Peggy regretted her decision.

Peggy walked away through the trees, then turned in the direction of their little paddock.

Micky'd load the stuff, she thought, and haul it away to Maguire's of Westport (under covers, naturally; one didn't want the excisemen or the peelers seeing). Old man Maguire would take the tea; Micky would get a large bag of money in return. When Micky got home she'd be wearing the red dress he liked. He'd have presents for her, ribbons, a hair clasp, a bracelet of gold. She'd have hot poítin punch made and they'd drink a bowl together. And the following Sunday, when she went to chapel, the ribbon round her bonnet, the clasp in her hair, the bracelet round her slim wrist, she'd outshine every other woman in the congregation . . .

"Hello," she called to the donkey who stood with his grey head hanging over the gate. He stood as if waiting to be harnessed. He always seemed to know when it was time to go to work . . .

When Micky got back from Maguire's, everything was exactly as Peggy had foreseen. Only Micky's mood wasn't right.

"Why so silent?" asked Peggy. "You should be happy with all that money in your pocket; you should be chattering away."

"I'm not unhappy," said Micky.

"What are you thinking about?"

"The Merrow . . ."⁹

At this point Mr Fee looked straight at me. 'In case you don't know, Merrow live in the sea. The males have green teeth, green hair, pig's eyes, and red noses. They're hideous. The women, on the other hand, are beautiful, for all their fish tails and the webbing between their fingers. All Merrow carry a cocked hat, usually red, and without this, they cannot go to their homes under the sea.'

Mr Rowley at Connor Street National School had told me of them too. The Merrow, he'd also said, were nasty and cruel and were never, under any circumstances, to be trusted. I nodded. Mr Fee smiled . . .

⁶ "My grandfather saw the Merrow all the time, didn't he?"

Micky said to Peggy. "And didn't he even want one to stand as godfather to his son, my own father? He only gave up the idea when the priest objected. And my father before me, though maybe not so friendly with the Merrow as his own father, he was no stranger to them either. Didn't he tell me?"

Peggy nodded.

"So how come then, though they're as plentiful as lobsters along this coast, I've never seen one?"

"I don't know. Maybe, they've gone to warmer seas."

"They were here long before us. They'll be here long after us."

Peggy said nothing. They brooded by the fire for a while and then they both went to bed.

One evening, a couple of weeks later, it was early spring now, Micky took a stroll along the coast. He was on a sandy path with a shingle and sand beach beside him, and the sea beyond. In the distance, at the other end of the beach, there was a rock standing proud of the sea, and on this rock, he suddenly saw somebody sitting.

"Who's that trespasser?" he exclaimed out loud.

Micky crept closer and it wasn't long before he saw, with its green body and a red cocked hat, it wasn't a man at all; it must be a Merrow.

He was amazed and delighted. A Merrow at last. He ran forward waving his arms and shouting.

The Merrow appeared to start at the sound of Micky's

voice. He stood up quickly and pulled his hat down hard on to his head. Then he dived head first from the rock, sliced through the water like a blade and vanished.

Micky was exasperated. However, Micky was not the sort who was put off easily, either.

The following evening, about the same time, Micky took his stick from the door.

"I'm going strolling," he said.

"A stroll? Why I might come with you."

But the Merrow were finicky and shy. If he saw the two of them, the Merrow might bolt. Micky stuck his nose out the door. "It's a bit miserable," he said.

"Is it?"

"Rain, I'd say."

"Is that so? Oh well," continued Peggy, settled with her knitting by the fire, "you go then. You won't be long, will you?"

"No," said Micky, and dashed away quickly before she could change her mind.

It was, in fact, a mild evening. The sky was pink along the horizon. The sea was a deep blue, almost the colour of ink. Swallows flitted in the air.

Micky reached the path by the shore. He squinted along the beach at the rock in the distance. It was small and dark and shaped like a lump of barley-sugar. And unmistakably, there on top, was a second smaller lump.

Micky began to gallop.

Then he stopped – dead.

He was close enough to see properly. No Merrow, Micky thought. He walked on, just to be certain but there was no Merrow. He'd just have to try another time.

"Haven't we become quite the evening walker," said Peggy, when he sallied out on the evening of the sixth or seventh day of his quest. "If I didn't trust and love you, I might almost think you were going out to meet a sweetheart."

"And who might that be?"

"A Merrow woman. The women are scaly but lovely and they prefer our sort to their own, as you would know because you told me so."

"I've never met with a Merrow, male or female, old or young, tall or small," said Micky, more or less truthfully, and with that he hurried off.

Poor Micky, once again he was disappointed. Perhaps there'd never been a Merrow at all, he thought. Yet Micky still continued to check the rock every evening.

Then there came a stormy night. A real wild one.

"You're not going out tonight, are you?" said Peggy, more than a little surprised.

"I just need to clear the old head," said Micky.

"I know one thing," said Peggy, "no woman would venture out in that."

"You're right there," said Micky and with that he fled.

The wind was gusting hard outside and Micky had to

half-close his eyes to keep out the bits of sandy grit that were blowing about.

The sea at his side was foaming and boiling, white and angry. Great drops of rain thudded into his face. Within seconds, the bones under his cheeks and along his chin had grown so cold, they hurt.

What on earth was he doing, Micky wondered? Why didn't he just turn round and go home to his warm soft wife sitting beside the big hot fire?

No, he'd go to the end of the beach. If the Merrow wasn't there, then Micky could turn round and go home. And if the Merrow was there, then Micky would know the satisfaction that comes when a man finally achieves what he has long struggled for.

Micky pushed on. What a storm.

Once at the end he peered through the dense sheets of spray thrown up by the action of the sea against the rock. He made out, just about, the barley-sugar outline but no second shape on top. Oh well, what did he expect, day like this? At least no one could accuse him of not trying. He had, oh he really had.

There was a small cave in the cliffs beyond. He would shelter there until the rain lifted.

Micky ran along the path. The entrance to the cave was dark and black, like a giant upside-down letter U carved into the bottom of the sheer rock cliff. The cave, the cave – that was all Micky thought of now.

With a sprint he finally made the entrance and dashed

in. He began to recover his breath. He was soaked to the skin.

"What a storm," said a voice.

Micky wondered why he was talking to himself. Then he realised he hadn't said a word. His heart raced. He looked round. The walls of the cave were dark with wet. Driftwood and rubbery strings of seaweed were piled higgledy-piggledy along the edges. In the middle of the cave there was a large round stone and someone was sitting on it.

It had a human shape. It had shoulders and a head, arms and legs. Then Micky saw the cocked hat. Then he saw the face. The teeth were green, the nose was red, the eyes, like those of a pig, were small dark liquorice discs held fast in a rim of pink skin, and the hair that hung down in a slick was green. The arms were short, like fins, and the bare legs were covered with scales and extending from the bottom of the back and flowing across the rock, was unmistakably a fish's tail.

Micky's mind worked quickly. He must adapt. He must charm. He must engage the Merrow in conversation.

"Your servant, sir," said Micky graciously. He doffed his cap and bowed from the waist.

"What a pleasure to meet you at last, young Micky Mealiffe."

"You know me!" he said, astounded.

"Yes."

"We've never met."

"No," the Merrow agreed. "But I know of you. I know who you are. I knew your grandfather, Fibber Mealiffe, long before he married Granny Hibbert. Oh yes, Fibber, a lovely man, you know. What am I saying. Of course you know, you were his grandson, weren't you."

"Indeed," said Micky, his thoughts racing.

"Your grandfather could knock back shellfuls of brandy like there was no tomorrow," said the Merrow. "I wonder, are you his match?"

"I wouldn't know," said Micky, modestly. This was a pretence but it might intrigue the Merrow; he might want to test Micky.

"You and I should become better acquainted," said the Merrow, staring blankly at Micky with his dark wet eyes.

"Yes," said Micky calmly, although he was so excited. His heart's desire was about to come true.

"For your grandfather's sake," continued the Merrow.

"Yes, I think we should," Micky agreed.

"But Micky, that father of yours, he had no head at all, had he?"

Micky decided to ignore this remark.

"Your honour," said Micky, ever so politely. "May I ask you a question?"

"A question is always free."

"The sea is so cold and you must often take brandy to warm yourself."

The Merrow nodded.

"And where would it be you come by this spirit?"

The Merrow laughed quietly. "The same as yourself. Some of it floats into your creek and some of it floats down to me. Or, I pop up and get it."

"Oh, I see."

"We are very alike."

Micky nodded, delighted. "And I suppose," continued Micky in his gentlest, most speculative voice, "you'd have a nice dry cellar where you'd keep your drink, and a nice dry pantry for your salt and your sugar, your bread and your tea, your butter and your honey."

"Oh yes," the Merrow agreed, "both of those and a great deal more besides."

Micky lifted his eyes and gazed wistfully at the roof of the cave.

"That would be something to see, I have no doubt, your cellar filled with dusty green bottles of brandy, your pantry filled with marvellous foods."

"You wouldn't know until you've seen it with your own eyes, the incomparable loveliness of my home at the bottom of the sea, with all the water of the ocean stacked overhead."

Micky found it impossible to picture. He wanted to see it himself very, very much. But he wasn't going to get an invitation if he asked.

"Meet me here next Monday at about this time," said the Merrow.

Micky nodded, indicating his agreement.

"We'll have a little talk."

The storm was still raging outside but Micky under-stood it was time to go. He doffed his cap and said goodbye and then walked quickly along the path.

When he reached home and went through the door, Peggy looked up from the corner. "You're soaked," she said.

"Just a little light spring storm. Bracing, invigorating, nothing to beat it."

Peggy came forward with a towel and wiped his face. "Micky Mealiffe," she said, "there must be a bit of the fish in you if you like being out in that."

Peggy began to towel his hair.

"Your grandfather maybe was married to a Merrow girl. Now get out of your wet togs and come over to the fire."

The following Monday evening, Micky took up his stick as usual.

"Having your walk?" asked Peggy.

"I noticed some gulls have nested near the bottom of the cliffs," he said.

Peggy waited.

"I might have a look in their nests. I might take an egg or two. Then again, I might not."

"So what is it you're saying?"

"I might just not be home when you expect."

"Ah," Peggy said. "Meeting our Merrow woman, are we?"

"No," said Micky. "Walking."

He hurried out of the house and along the path towards the cave. The sea was calm.

Micky reached the cave. He went in. "Good evening," said Micky.

"Good evening."

The Merrow was sitting on the rock exactly as the first time they met. Perhaps he hadn't moved? Oh, but yes, he had.

"You have, I notice, two cocked hats," said Micky.

"I have."

"Is it for me to have a try of one," said Micky, laughing, "since it's so curiously shaped?" He said this in his dissembling voice; he knew perfectly well why the Merrow had two.

"I don't come by these hats so easily," the Merrow said, tartly. "And I certainly wouldn't give one away to someone because I believed they might be amused by its shape."

"'Course you wouldn't," said Micky quickly.

"I want you to come down and have dinner with me. I brought you the hat so you can do that."

Micky smiled. "You want me to go down to the bottom of the sea," he said, mock incredulously. "But I can't do that. My lungs will fill with water, I'll drown, and poor Peggy will be left a widow with no husband to care for her."

"Your grandfather would never have spoken like that," said the Merrow. "Do you know what he'd have said? 'Yes please, I'm coming to dinner!' Then he'd have grabbed this very hat, jammed it on his head, and dived down into the sea . . ."'

Suddenly, Mr Fee stopped and stared around the carriage, just like Mr Rowley when he read stories. I heard the iron wheels clattering below the floor. I saw the flat Irish midlands stretching away, the Royal Canal in the distance, a straight ribbon of dark water. Then Mr Fee opened his mouth and I made ready to drop down into the story world again . . .

'Micky didn't let on but he was smarting. He had always admired his grandfather but apparently, if the Merrow was to be believed, the old fellow would have found his grandson to be cautious and over-domesticated.

"Give it here," Micky exclaimed, and he reached forward and snatched the cocked hat.

"That's what I like! Now come along and do as I do."

They left the cave and walked into the sea. They swam out to the rock. The Merrow climbed up on to it. Micky climbed after him. Then the Merrow crossed the rock and looked down, and Micky followed suit.

Remember how I said this rock, seen from the beach, was shaped like a barley-sugar. But on the far side, the sea side, there was nothing but a sheer drop, straight down into a sea so deep, it made Micky's head spin just to gaze down into it.

"You put on the hat," explained the Merrow, "you jump

in. You open your eyes, you get hold of my tail. I'll do the rest."

The Merrow plunged down into the green sea.

For a second Micky wavered. But if he let this chance slip through his fingers, he'd always regret it.

He jammed the hat over his ears and jumped in. Micky felt the sea pushing against his open eyes. The Merrow swam on, Micky trailed behind. The water got colder and darker. Micky was vaguely aware of fish flashing past but his entire attention was on the tail that he held with one hand, and the hat on his head which he held in place with the other. Micky knew that without the hat he would drown, and in a few days his body would be washed into his creek, where Peggy would find it.

Eventually, Micky found himself on dry land at the bottom of the sea, standing in front of a nice white house neatly slated with oyster shells. Smoke was coming out of the chimney.

"My house," said the Merrow with great dignity. "You are most welcome."

Micky looked around. Crabs and lobsters scuttled along the dry sandy floor. The sea, which stretched above, was like the sky (except it was grey and green rather than blue) and fishes, like birds, were swimming around in it.

"Lost our tongue?" asked the Merrow. "Or perhaps we're fretting about Peggy," he added mischievously, "and we want to go straight back home and sit with our wife by the hearth."

"I'm filled with wonder," replied Micky, which was the truth.

"Come on."

The Merrow led Micky into the kitchen. There was a stove, a dresser covered with good-looking plates and two young Merrow chopping up vegetables.

The Merrow led Micky to another room. For a table, a wide rough plank rested between two stones covered with wisps of dry seaweed and dry barnacles, and for seats there were up-ended logs. There was a fire blazing away in the hearth.

"Let me show you a sight for sore eyes," the Merrow said.

He led Micky down a corridor, through a door, down some stairs where cobwebs stretched between the bannister rails, and finally into a small dark room which smelt of old stone. On the brick shelves there were bottles piled, bottles of every colour, bottles covered in dust and more cobwebs.

"Who says a Merrow can't be cosy under the ocean?"

"I never thought it for a second," said Micky, quietly.

His mind was racing. He'd never imagined himself in the Merrow's home, in his cellar. And now he had seen the world at the bottom of the sea, he would tell neither Peggy nor anyone else. Not even when he lay on his deathbed.

"You look pensive," said the Merrow.

"It's nothing," Micky said. "It's just I keep thinking I'm

going to wake up and all this will have been a dream."

"No, it's not," the Merrow said.

"I know it's not."

"I don't think I'll have wine tonight. Do you mind?"

"Why should I mind?" said Micky.

"Wine will be too cold on my stomach, tonight," the Merrow said, suddenly sounding like a fussy old gentleman.

The Merrow went back to the room with the fire. Micky followed him. Dinner was now laid on the planks. There were platters of fish and a basket of oysters on a bed of seaweed.

Micky sat and ate. When he was finished eating, he filled a shell with brandy and raised it.

"Your honour," he said formally, "I'd like to toast your health, although isn't it mighty odd, I don't know your name."

"That's true, Micky, it is, but better late than never, as they say; my name is Coomara."

"Coomara. What a fine and lovely name," Micky continued enthusiastically. "Here's to your health and may you have another fifty years as good as the last."

"Fifty!" exclaimed Coomara. "Just fifty?"

Micky had the unpleasant sense that his evening was about to go wrong.

"Fifty, well, I say fifty, ah . . .?"

"Fifty is marvellous," said Coomara, "but five hundred would be a better wish."

"My goodness, you do live for a long time down here.

You knew my grandfather and he's been dead a lock of years, and you knew my father."

"Not quite as well," interrupted Coomara.

"It must be healthier down here than up there."

Coomara smiled benignly. More shells of brandy were poured. More toasts were drunk. Then songs were sung. Finally, Coomara said to Micky, "Now, my dear boy, if you follow me, I will show you my curiosities!"

Coomara went over to the corner of the room where there was a small low door. It was in shadow and until this moment Micky hadn't noticed it. Coomara produced a large black key from his waistcoat pocket and unlocked the door.

"Come on, Micky," he called, and ducking low, Coomara disappeared into the room beyond.

Micky hurried after him. Perhaps the room was filled with jewels or gold. This idea excited Micky. At the same time he felt just a little anxious.

Micky ducked down under the lintel and found himself in a long barn. Lanterns, coils of rope and hawser, oars and fishing nets lay everywhere. There was even a boat on rollers.

Coomara picked his way through the clutter and went straight to the wall. Here, stacked along the entire length of the wall, piled from the floor right up to the ceiling, stood what looked to Micky like lobster-pots.

"Well, what do you make of my curiosities?" Coomara asked.

"Well, they're very . . ." For a second Micky was lost for words. "They look like lobster-pots, but they aren't, are they, quite?"

"No," Coomara agreed.

"What are they then?"

"Soul cages."

"Soul cages?"

"Uh-huh."

"What's a soul cage for?"

"It's a cage for keeping souls in," said Coomara, as if only an imbecile could fail to know something so obvious.

"For keeping souls?" said Micky. He felt a distant but nonetheless quite distinct prickle of anxiety in the mysterious region behind the solar plexus, where his conscience always troubled him. "Umh, what souls would that be?" continued Micky, ungrammatically. "There's no soul in a fish or any other creature in the ocean, is there?"

"Agreed," said Coomara, "but it's the souls of drowned sailors I keep in these things."

Micky was at a loss for words. He felt as if a knife had sliced through him. Whence came these souls? Obviously, from the ships that sunk because they were tripped up, so to speak, by the rock that stuck out like a leg into the sea. Was Micky the cause? Well no, he was in the clear there. Yet he did nothing to stop it, just like his father and his grandfather before him. And the odd life he had saved didn't alter the essential fact that he now understood for the first time: there was blood on his hands. Others died that he might prosper and flourish. And their souls were kept by Coomara, safe and snug, in his wretched cages, far from the sight or grace of God.

Of course, Coomara shouldn't do as he did, but he was a Merrow and he didn't know better. Micky did know better; he was a man. The problem now was what should he do?

The answer was obvious. Release the souls. But how? He could drown in the process, or get caught, or fail. Yet if he didn't his conscience would torment him until he did its bidding. And that was an even more terrifying idea – the contemplation of the pain he would suffer until he acted.

These cataclysmic upheavals in his soul happened in less than a second. Micky began to shake. Then he rallied.

"Ah yes," said Micky, calmly. "How do you get them?"

If he let Coomara have sight of his conscience now, the Merrow might take steps to stop him acting, or later, after Micky had acted, he might realise the culprit was Micky.

"Oh, easy," said the Merrow, expansively. "We get a good storm. The ships blow in from the Atlantic. They trip up on that leg of rock – you know it well, of course. The ship sinks, the mariners are cast in the water. They drown. Their souls float free. It's cold, it's confusing in the sea but my pots are there. The souls sneak in, it's warm and snug in these pots, but once in, of course, they can't get out. I bring them home. And here I keep them, in the dry and warmth. And isn't it well they have such good quarters?"

"Oh yes," Micky agreed hastily.

The two friends went back to the dining-room to drink several more shellfuls of brandy.

"It's getting a bit late," said Micky. "I'm worried about Peggy."

"Why, what's there to worry about. She's your wife, she's at home, what's the matter?"

"I'm not worried about anything precisely, I'm just worried she might be anxious because I'm not home yet."

Coomara nodded. "You've a long journey and a cold one. Have this," he said.

Micky knew better than to refuse. He took the shell and swallowed the liquor. "Will I find my way back?"

"Why wouldn't you? Won't I put you on your way?"

Coomara took down a cocked hat from a hook on the wall. Then he went out into the garden and Micky followed him. Coomara put the hat on Micky's head but this time he put it on back to front. Then he got Micky up on to his shoulder.

"I'm going to throw you up here," Coomara said, "and you'll come out at the very spot where you dived in from the rock. Mind you throw me back the hat – and by the way, you can always throw a stone down from that same spot if you ever want to reach me – and then go you home."

Micky felt Coomara pushing from below and himself rising upwards like a cork from a bottle. Suddenly, he was on the rock, feet apart and arms out, ready to dive, just exactly as he was when he had started. He took off the hat and threw it down. It hit the water with a splash and sank from sight like a stone.

In the distance, Micky saw the sun was sinking. He swam lazily to the shore. Once on land he shook himself like a dog and emptied the salt water from his boots. Then he began to walk home. He heard a curlew call – a melancholy sound. Never in his wildest dreams had Micky imagined that he would visit the home of the Merrow and that the Merrow would show him his soul cages. In one part of himself Micky wished he had never started this. Now he would have to do something.

The sun had fallen below the horizon by the time Micky reached the front door of his cabin. He took off his jacket and hung it on a hook by the window. It was the hook, he reminded himself grimly, which he used to hang his own lobster-pots.

Micky went inside the cabin.

"Hello to you, husband," said Peggy, looking up from the hearth.

Micky closed the door behind him. Peggy made no noise as she crossed the floor. She touched his arm. His shirt was wet.

"You're wet," she said.

"Am I? Oh . . . yes. I fell . . . in the sea . . . in the creek . . . out of the boat . . ."

He turned and opened the door and rushed back outside to retrieve his jacket.

"Got to dry this," he said, hurrying back in.

Peggy thought her husband was in an odd mood but said nothing. She made tea and they drank it in silence. Later, they went to bed and lay, quite still in the darkness, with their backs turned to one another.

Peggy knew something was up and she would get to the bottom of it, or her name wasn't Mrs Micky Mealiffe.

Micky, meanwhile, with his mind's eye, saw one of the soul cages floating in front of him. Under the sea, Micky hadn't doubted that inside each wicker prison there was a soul in torment. But was it not possible that the cages were empty?

Ah, but they would look empty, wouldn't they, came the reply from the part of him that was ready and willing to do the right thing. The soul had no colour, shape, smell or taste. The soul was invisible to ordinary mortals. Only God could see who or what was trapped inside them, only God and Coomara.

It couldn't be right, of course, keeping them locked up like that. When a man died, his soul went to heaven where it was reunited with the original maker of the world. Life on earth might be a misery, but the life that came after made up for that. Except in the case of these poor sailors, that was; the sweet afterlife of grace was not their fate.

And for all Micky knew, Coomara would keep them in the soul cages for the rest of eternity. Never, ever would they know the joy of standing in the presence of God.

So he was going to act the hero, was he, the furtive part of his nature piped up, and get into God knows what kind of trouble?

While Micky trembled at the idea of the task ahead, the old Adam in his soul threw out a new idea. Why not go to the priest?

In his mind's eye Micky imagined Father Joseph at the door of the parochial house and himself on the doorstep. He heard the priest saying, 'What is it?' then saw his mouth opening and closing and a look of appalled disbelief spreading over Father Joseph's long pale face.

Oh so what if he doesn't believe you! This was Micky's conscience again. He, Micky he was the one who had seen; therefore, he was the one who must act. It was that simple. He must forget the priest. Coomara didn't care a fig for him and anyway, what was Father Joseph going to do even if he were to believe?

There was, besides, another compelling reason not to speak to the cleric. It would lead to questions. Why had Micky gone looking for the Merrow, for instance? This, in turn, might lead to the business of his grandfather's past association with the Merrow coming out. Father Joseph was a man who liked to know everything. No, the cleric was not an option.

Micky felt a small glow of pleasure. The weasel in him

had come up with the priest and Micky'd seen the idea off. He still had a conscience. He would have to act, and act alone.

For a few minutes various stupid ideas swirled around in Micky's head.

Then a new idea floated into his mind. The longer he thought about it, the better it seemed.

He closed his eyes and, a few seconds later, he fell fast asleep.

When Micky woke a couple of hours later, it was still dark. He coughed and lay looking up at the ceiling.

The dawn came, and light began to show around the edges of the shutters that covered the single tiny window.

Micky coughed again and wriggled about. Eventually, as he had intended, Peggy woke up.

"Good morning, husband," she said.

Micky felt Peggy's leg snake across the bed and then her foot rubbing up and down his shin.

"Wife?" he said.

"Yes, my darling."

"What are you doing?"

"I'm rubbing your shin before I . . ."

"I've been thinking," said Micky.

"What is it, my love?"

Peggy slid across the bed towards him. Micky slid away from her towards the edge.

"I've been thinking that we haven't yet had the blessing

of a child," he said boldly. He felt Peggy stop her sliding and lift her head from the pillow the better to hear what he had to say.

"I had a dream last night," he continued.

"Of our child was it that you dreamt?" said Peggy. She spoke in a new, softer voice. Peggy wanted a child; she had wanted a child for a while now.

"No," said Micky, carefully, "not our child. No, I dreamt you were at St. John's Well at Ennis, and that after you came home we were blessed with a child."

"Did you, my darling?" said Peggy. She lent over and kissed him chastely on the mouth. "If you've had such a dream, then it would seem I'll have to go."

After breakfast, Peggy got out her best bonnet and changed the ribbon by which it tied under her chin from red (rather too eye-catching, she thought) to grey (better, more chaste). She unpacked her dark walking dress and cleaned the hem and the buttons. She hung her shawl in front of the fire to air. She cleaned her six-eye walking boots and ironed a pair of grey stockings with white stays. She made eight loaves of soda bread so Micky would not go hungry while she was away. She mixed up three stone of Indian meal so all Micky would have to do was throw the chickens their feed in the morning and the evening. She washed Micky's best shirt and hung it out to dry. It would be ready for her to iron when she got back on Saturday, so he could wear it when they went to Mass together on Sunday. She swept the hearth and the floor.

She scrubbed the table with hot water. She dusted the windowsills and the door-lintel and the St Brigid's Cross.

Housekeeping completed, she went out to the spring at the back. The water collected in a pool underneath the spring before it ran off into the sea.

Peggy stripped to the buff and jumped in, taking care not to wet her hair. (She only washed her hair twice a year, on Christmas Eve and Midsummer Eve, with a mixture of egg white and lemon juice.)

Peggy scrubbed herself around the body quickly with a handful of sand, jumped out, dried herself, dressed herself, ran home. She changed her earrings. She dabbed flour on her cheeks and a little rouge on her lips. She found her prayer book and her rosary and packed them in a dolly-bag with a nightgown, a spare shawl, her brush-and-comb set and her rouge. She opened the money tin and took out two white five pound notes (these were strictly for emergencies) two sovereigns, two shillings, two sixpences and eight coppers. She put the money in the purse and she put the purse in the deepest part of the pocket of her walking dress.

The cart was ready and waiting for her at the door and Micky was sitting up on the front seat with the reins in his hands. Peggy's straw-filled sack, on which she always sat, was already laid out for her in the back of the cart.

"You're a considerate man, Micky Mealiffe," she said as she got up. What a wise choice she had made when she chose to marry him.

"Giddy-up," said Micky as he shook the reins.

The donkey ambled around the house and along the coast road and arrived eventually in the town. A few people were already waiting by the courthouse for the Ennis diligence. Micky pulled up. Peggy bought a first-class return in Finagh's Grocery shop. This would allow her to sit inside.

"You'll meet me here Saturday, won't you Micky?" she said when she came back.

"I promise."

"And you'll think of me fondly while I'm away?"

"Oh, yes."

He seemed distracted. Did he mind her going away? He'd never minded before when she'd gone on pilgrimages.

"Goodbye," said Micky. He smiled and showed her his nice even teeth.

No, Peggy thought. It was her imagination. There was nothing to worry about. She would go, she would make her penance, she would come home. And, with any luck, God would grant her dearest wish.

Arriving home, Micky took the donkey out from between the shafts and put him in the paddock. He took the tackle into the meal-house to clean later. Then he went into the kitchen. He cut himself a thick slice from one of the new loaves and as the slice fell sideways, a wreath of steam rose up. He dug a piece of cheddar out of the truckle and put it on the bread. Some men worked best on an empty stomach, but not Micky.

He went down to the beach and, chewing his bread and cheese, he walked along to the rock. There was no sign of Coomara. But then, they had no plans to meet, had they?

He bent down and selected a stone. He walked down the shelving beach and out into the sea. The water was calm and very still. Patches of foam floated on the surface. They looked like milk bubbles, Micky thought.

The water was up to his waist. He picked a fleck of cheese from between two teeth and swallowed it, then leant gently forward and began to swim. Wasn't it well for him his grandfather had taught him how to do this? Wasn't it odd, too, that his father did not swim? Perhaps his grandfather deliberately did not teach his father to swim so he could not associate with the Merrow?

This led to the next thought. Coomara must have minded when he was stood down as godfather. It was after all his way into human society. Maybe the resentment he felt, following on from this, took the form of a reticence that came in time to seem like dislike.

The rock loomed ahead. He scrambled up to the top. He took the stone out of his pocket. He walked to the far side that fell away like a wall, and lined the stone up above the spot where he had thrown the hat. Then he let go the stone; it fell, made a splash and vanished into the dark blue water.

Micky looked at the sea spread at his feet. It rose and

then fell, gently. It was exactly the same motion as Peggy made when she was sleeping beside him.

Deep in the blue he saw something coming up towards him, blurred at first, then clearer and clearer.

"Good afternoon, Micky," said Coomara, bursting out of the sea like a cork from a pop gun. He wore his cocked hat back to front. "I got your rock. What is it?"

He sounded slightly testy.

"Oh," said Micky in his most genial tone of voice. "It's nothing really, nothing, it's nothing; it's just my house is empty tonight, the woman's gone away on pilgrimage and the mice, I thought, could play, while the cat is away."

Coomara tilted his head sideways. "What exactly is it you had in mind?"

"A little dinner, a little brandy, a pipe or two of tobacco, a convivial evening."

"I would be delighted to accept your offer," said Coomara, expansively. "Delighted. I spent many happy hours in that cabin. It will be most agreeable to relive those happy times."

"Until tonight," said Micky.

"Eight o'clock?"

"Eight o'clock."

Coomara turned his hat so the front faced forwards; then he dived into the sea and vanished. Micky turned, walked back across the rock, jumped into the water and swam to the beach. He'd achieved the most difficult part of the enterprise. All he had to do was get Coomara senseless with drink, "borrow" his cocked hat, nip down to the bottom of the sea, open the cages and hey presto! Simple really.

That afternoon, Micky caught himself a beautiful sleek sea salmon, a male. It had a lovely pink belly, and a fine grey back with beautiful inky black spots dotted across it.

He cleaned the fish in the sea, brought him home, packed the carcass in clay and put him in the embers of the fire to cook slowly. He fetched two bottles of his very best brandy from the roof space of the meal shed. Micky washed the ancient bottles, then wiped the glass dry until it shone. He pulled the corks out and put his nose to the opening. A keen thin smell rose into his face and spread down the back of his throat. It was sharp and intense and his head swam.

Coomara was at the door at eight, exactly. The salmon came up from the embers in his crisp coat of mud. The coat was unbuttoned and a marvellous smell of sea salt and wet salmon flesh filled the little cabin.

"One for you and one for me," said Micky, pushing a bottle across the table towards his guest.

"You are a generous soul," said Coomara expansively.

When Micky was courting Peggy, at the very mention of her name, his temperature rose and his blood sped more quickly around his body, and now, at the mention of the word soul, Micky's face flushed and his heart began to beat. Coomara had fathomed his thoughts! Otherwise, why would Coomara have said soul, like that?

Micky kept his red face tilted towards the table but raised his eyes. He expected to find the Merrow staring at him and was relieved to see Coomara was carefully filling his glass with brandy. Micky felt his face cooling. He had not been caught out . . .

In the hours that followed, Coomara ate and drank manfully. All seemed to be going well until Coomara announced, tipping his bottle completely upside-down "It's empty, I've drunk it all."

He then looked across the table and saw the level in Micky's bottle hadn't even got below the neck. "You're drinking very little," said Coomara. "I could be forgiven for thinking you want to see me addled."

Coomara's small eyes suddenly looked quite malevolent. Their colour changed from green to amber.

"I'll get you another," said Micky quickly, "now yours is empty." He rushed off to his store and fetched a third bottle. When he got back he didn't wash off the cobwebs or the dust. He just uncorked the bottle and gave it straight to his guest.

"You should be keeping pace with me," said Coomara, belligerently.

"I'm not the Merrow you are," said Micky slyly. "I'm just a mere man. I can only take a little."

"Don't be so ridiculous," said Coomara. His pig eyes were bright red now. "You're the grandson of a man who could drink me under the table. I don't hold with this mealy-mouthed stuff. Drink up, come on."

What if Coomara took offence, grabbed his hat and rushed back to his underwater world, never to return? Then Micky'd never be able to get down to the cages to free the imprisoned souls. He would be in a kind of hell, for ever.

"Why," said Micky heartily, "I've been tardy but I'm going to get some of this into me now." He tipped the bottle over his glass and brandy glugged out. "To my friend, Coomara," he exclaimed, and raised the glass. "And may we have many more marvellous evenings like this."

He saw Coomara was watching him closely. He took a gulp. Coomara still stared. He took another. Then a third. Coomara smiled. He had convinced Coomara there was nothing to worry about.

Unfortunately, Micky now felt light-headed. He knew that what he had hoped to do was no longer possible. He should have thought this through.

He and the Merrow talked and sang and drank. It grew late. Finally, Coomara took a fob from his waistcoat pocket and squinted at the face.

"It's nearly midnight," he said. "I never realised it was that late. That was a lovely evening. I must go home now." Coomara took his hat from the hook on the back of the door and put it on his head.

"Would you not prefer to sleep here?" Micky suggested, "and go home in the morning? I can make you up a nice comfortable bed in front of the fire."

"Another night, my dear friend. Tonight I must go home."

Micky opened the door. "Will you take a lantern with you, to light your way?" he said quickly.

"How will I get it back to you?"

"You'll be coming again. You can give it back then." Micky rushed back into the cabin and emerged with a lantern.

"Thank you," said Coomara, taking the handle. He set off down the path whistling as he went. After a few moments Coomara's bulky shape became invisible, but Micky watched the small frail flame bobbing along until Coomara passed beyond the pine trees. Then Micky went back inside, fell into bed and, after hurriedly running through his prayers, fell instantly asleep.

The next morning, after breakfast, he hitched the donkey and went off along the coast road in the opposite direction to town; the road took him to a part of the country that was even wilder and more lonely than where he lived. Finally, he arrived at his destination, a small, crooked, miserable cabin beside a black pond.

He pulled on the reins and put on the brake. He sat and waited. After a few minutes he heard bolts being drawn. The door opened and an old woman looked out. This was Biddy.

"Two," called Micky.

Biddy scowled. She came out and closed the door grumpily behind her. She padded off along the path to an outhouse in her bare feet. A few minutes later she came up to the side of the cart again, carrying two bottles of poítin that was indistinguishable from water to the naked eye.

"Pay," she demanded.

Micky handed Biddy two shillings, warm from his palm. "Is it good poítin?" he asked as he took the bottles. He held one up to the light.

"I just sell it, I don't drink it," said Biddy in a surly voice.

"Oh dear. We're not our usual happy self today, are we?"

"Where's the empties?"

"Sorry," said Micky, blinking with mock innocence. "I forgot them. I'll bring them next time."

"I'm not a charity." Inside her small creased brown mouth, her small teeth sloped inwards. "Come on, pay for those bottles, you know my rules."

Micky sighed theatrically. "Biddy, you are not a generous soul." He got out the two pennies he'd brought in readiness and tossed them at her. Biddy caught them.

"Go away now, Micky Mealiffe, get off my property before the excisemen see you hanging round my door and put two and two together." She walked down the path jingling the money.

"As always, a pleasure," Micky called.

He shook the reins and the donkey moved off pulling the rumbling cart behind.

As soon as he got home Micky swam out to the rock with a stone in his pocket. He dropped it in the usual spot. A few moments later Coomara rose out of the water and a second after, he was standing in front of Micky as bold as brass.

"I have your lantern at home still," said the Merrow. "How thoughtless of me. I should have realised you were up here and brought it up with me."

Coomara's ways were gentlemanly, Micky thought, whereas what he was embarked on was in no way gentlemanly. Yet he must save those souls.

"You hold on to that lantern because you may need it again," said Micky.

"Why would that be?"

"With the cat still away, shouldn't the mice have another play? Come round this evening, at eight. I promise I'll be as high spirited as my grandfather. Tonight it's a new Micky you'll see," he boasted. "My grandfather wouldn't be able to hold a candle to me if he was still with us."

"Oh," said Coomara. "I definitely will have to come then, won't I?"

Coomara reversed his cocked hat and dived back into the sea.

Micky knelt down and took his knife from his pocket. Then he made a series of small marks on the surface of the rock, at the exact point where Coomara had stood before launching himself forward.

Micky caught a dozen lovely fat codfish that afternoon. He hung them upside down over the fire to cook. For hours the fish juices dripped down and hissed on the embers. He wiped clean the poítin bottles and uncorked them. He cleaned the empties he'd not returned to Biddy and filled them with water. He was ready.

At eight Coomara appeared with his cocked hat under his arm and Micky's lantern.

"Is this the house of Micky Mealiffe?" he asked, "who says he's as good a man as his grandfather?"

"Come in, esteemed guest," Micky said, pretending to be a lord.

Coomara bustled in, hung his hat on the hook, put the lantern on the table, and sat down.

"For you," said Micky, pushing the two opened bottles of poítin towards his guest. "And these are mine." He pointed at the two bottles of water on the dresser. "Now let me see if I can manage to come even half-way up to my grandfather's measure." He took a bottle, filled his glass, and swallowed the contents in four impressive gulps.

"My goodness," said Coomara.

It was hard to judge if this was admiration or envy.

"I only saw your grandfather drink poítin once," said Coomara, "when he had ague, and he didn't drink it like that, I remember."

"How did he drink it?"

"He sipped it. It's a very strong drink, isn't it?"

"Oh, yes."

"We never get it down where I am. When I saw your grandfather sipping it (I had a brandy by the way) I asked for a taste but he wouldn't give me one. Oh, go on, I said. He shook his head. I asked him a few more times after that but he always said no. Eventually, he explained that unlike wine or brandy, poítin was really a medicine and as such wasn't a fit drink for a guest. After that I never asked him for a taste again."

"So it follows, I suppose, you wouldn't know how to manage it?" said Micky blithely.

"I'm sorry. What exactly are you saying?"

"I can knock it back because I'm used to it, whereas not having any practice, you'll have to be very careful this evening."

"I can manage my drink very well, thank you very much."

"Of course," said Micky quickly. "I don't mean to cause offence. I'm just saying, you're not used to it. And as one who knows what it's like, let me give some advice to my dear guest who doesn't, by his own admission, know what it's like. Treat her with respect, go slowly. Master the drink, don't let her master you."

"I see," replied Coomara.

He spoke quietly too but, deep down, Coomara was angry, as Micky intended. Now, it was a point of principle

75

with Coomara that there was no drink on earth he was not able to manage. He was determined he'd prove to this young whippersnapper (who certainly didn't have his grandfather's manners) that he could drink him under the table.

"I think," said Coomara, "it's time I took my first draught."

He filled his glass, then drank off the whole lot in a single gulp; then he loudly exclaimed, "My goodness," and shuddered involuntarily.

"My goodness, I don't think I could manage to take a full glass just like that, in a single swipe," said Micky, admiringly. "I needed several goes to get my last glass down."

He filled his own glass again with water. He tipped his head back and swallowed the water down in a single gasping gulp, then slammed his glass down on the table and shouted, "Yahoo. Say, if you dare, that I'm not my grandfather's grandson, now."

Coomara coldly filled his own glass with poítin. This time he filled it right up to the brim. He swallowed the lot. A second later he let out a hoarse gasp.

"Capital!" Micky shouted in his lordly voice.

"Whew!" replied Coomara.

"That was some drink," said Micky. "Come on, again."

Micky filled his glass with water. Coomara filled his glass with poítin. The two drained their glasses simultaneously.

"Again," said Micky.

They repeated and repeated the action until all of the first and half of the second bottle of poítin was gone.

Coomara's face was bright, bright red. He was sweating. His movements were unsteady. His eyes were hazy and unfocused.

"An . . . other? An . . . other?" cried Micky, taking care to appear drunk. He filled Coomara's glass with poítin and his own with water. "To my dear friend, Coomara." Micky raised his glass.

Coomara stared blankly.

Micky leaned over.

"Come on, I'll help you, friend." He reached over, took the glass out of Coomara's hand and lifted the glass to Coomara's lips. "Come on, drink."

Any second now, Micky thought. When the glass was empty Micky whipped it away and with his other, free hand, he caught the Merrow's head. The eyelids were shut tight. He lowered the Merrow's heavy fishy head on to the scrubbed table top. He listened to the Merrow's slow heavy breathing. He was out cold. Alleluia.

Micky swung the crane with the fish away from the fire. He put a fresh candle in the lantern, grabbed Coomara's cocked hat and rushed out.

When he arrived at the beach, Micky set the lantern down in a sheltered spot. Holding the cocked hat clamped between his teeth, he swam out to the foot of rock that stuck out into the water and climbed up on to the rock. He felt for the tiny nicks he had made with his knife. He put his feet on the marks and stood up. He pulled the cocked hat on to his head and pitched himself forward.

Micky felt himself striking the water, then falling, falling, falling. He was moving through utter blackness and darkness until, suddenly, he hit solid ground with a bump that winded him. He was lying, flat on his back in Coomara's front garden, staring at the dark night sea above . . .

He found the path and made his way down to the door. He opened the latch and went in. Not a Merrow to be seen.

Micky felt along the sill of the window nearest the door and found a candle holder. He went to the hearth and lit the stub that was stuck in it.

He made his way to the big room. It was quiet and still as the crypt of a church. He walked to the first wicker cage. There was a small door at the front that was held fast with a pin that dropped through a round of wire.

Micky pulled back the pin and opened the door. He heard a ghostly whoosh. It was like the noise made by wind as it rushes up a flue, only quieter and of shorter duration.

He closed the cage and sealed it shut. No point letting Coomara know his prisoners had escaped.

Micky walked the entire way round the room, opening door after door and releasing soul after soul. By the time he got back to the point where he started, his arm felt quite tired, while in his heart he felt remarkably cheerful. He had done kind deeds before but nothing on this scale. Tonight he had freed hundreds of souls. Alleluia.

Micky padded back to the kitchen. He blew the candle out and set it back on the sill, exactly where he found it. Exactly. With luck, Coomara might never realise what had happened.

Micky went outside. This was the hour before dawn. The quietest hour of the night.

The question now was, how did he get up into the sea again? His heart beating, Micky went round the side of the cottage. He'd find a ladder, somewhere, surely?

But Micky didn't even have to start looking. As he came round into Coomara's yard, he saw the sea dipped slightly here and so was just within his reach. He went forward towards the dip. At that very moment, a fat codfish, swimming lazily past, let its tail dangle down into the air immediately below.

Micky acted without thinking. He reversed the cocked hat. He jumped up and grabbed the cod's tail.

The cod, feeling Micky's hand grasping his tail, shrieked with shock and surprise and bolted upwards, in the process pulling Micky after himself up into the sea.

A second later Micky realised there was water all around him. At the same moment, the cod turned and looked to see what was holding his tail.

"Oh ye gods and fishes," exclaimed the cod. It was the

very same man who'd hooked his brothers the day before and now, horror of horrors, this same man had caught him.

Micky released the cod. The fish was hugely relieved and swam away to the coldest, deepest water it knew. Micky shot upwards like a ball from a cannon, and landed, feet first, on the rock. He saw that the candle burned still in the lantern.

He jumped back into the sea on the landward side and swam to the shore. When he got out he was cold. He was also happy. He picked up the lantern. He must get to his cabin before Coomara woke.

Micky ran all the way to his door. A pale light glimmered along the edge of the horizon. Dawn was about to break.

He stopped quite still. Could he hear Coomara? No. He pushed the door back silently. Thank goodness. Coomara was exactly where Micky had left him, head on the table, making the Merrow equivalent of a snore.

Micky crept in and closed the door noiselessly. He removed the cocked hat and placed it carefully on the hook. He went to the fire and packed clods around the embers.

Then he slipped into the little bedroom. He took off his wet clothes and put on dry ones.

Micky was exhausted. He looked at his bed which stretched beside him, invitingly. Couldn't he just lie down for a few minutes?

* * *

"What on earth . . . my God . . . Micky . . ."

Micky sat straight up. His heart was beating. He scrambled to his feet, bounded across the room and threw the door open.

"Peggy," he shouted.

His wife stood on the other side of the room.

"Micky, what is that?" she asked furiously and pointed at Coomara, lying with his head on her scrubbed table.

"That's my friend."

"Your friend."

"My very good friend, Coomara."

"That's not a friend, that's a disgusting creature of some sort."

At this moment, Coomara sat up and stared around with his small pig eyes. He did look awful. "Hello. Where am I?"

"You're in my cabin,"

"Oh," said the Merrow.

"It's the morning."

"Oh. Was I asleep all night?"

"Yes."

"Ah."

"And this is my wife," said Micky.

Coomara turned and caught Peggy scowling in his direction.

"Madame," he said, standing and then burping, "I know we've only just met, but I must say goodbye."

He took his hat. "My dear friend, Micky, you are your grandfather's son. Drop a stone next time you're at the rock." He stepped out into the morning, closing the door behind.

"Peggy, you're early," said Micky.

"Yes. I caught last night's diligence. I walked from town this morning."

Peggy went over to the crane with the fat cod hanging from it.

"Are you hungry?"

Micky said he was. She swung the crane over the fire to heat up the fish. She put on the blackened kettle to boil up some water for tea.

"How was the pilgrimage?" asked Micky.

Peggy smiled. "Unnecessary. I will be having a baby but I didn't find out until I got to Ennis. Once I knew, there was no need to finish the pilgrimage. I came home and glad I am that I did. I won't be leaving you alone again in a hurry now I know what you get up to when I'm away."

"Yes," agreed Micky, nodding.

They ate a breakfast of codfish and sweet hot tea. Afterwards, Micky said it was the best breakfast he'd ever had. This was his first direct comment on the news that he was going to be a father and Peggy understood this.

That afternoon, when it was fine, and the sea was still and milky, Micky went out in his little boat with a pile of flotation buoys. He anchored the buoys, at intervals, along the wall of rock running out into the sea. That night he wrote a letter to the coastguard and advised them of the wall of rock. Peggy read the letter. She said nothing. She was a superstitious soul, as well as a religious one, who believed that nothing on this earth was given but something else was taken away. She had been given a baby so it was obvious that she and Micky would have to renounce their old ways.

The coastguard received Micky's letter. In just a few weeks the maps were altered and permanent warning buoys placed at sea. No ship would ever founder again and Micky would never harvest another floating cargo. He would have to live by other means – and that meant fishing. It was arduous but Micky worked hard, he learnt quickly, and every day he was filled with the sublime feeling that for once in his life he had actually done what was right. There was less money in the Mealiffe household, it was true, but he was happy and so was Peggy. A child, they both realised, was something on which no value could ever be placed. What they had given up was as nothing compared to what they were going to receive.

As for Coomara, he never missed those souls he had caged up. He and Micky remained the best of friends. When the baby was born, Micky insisted his friend must stand as godfather and this time, he said, the priest would not be given the opportunity to turn Coomara down. Peggy (who was reconciled, by this stage, to the Merrow) dressed him in a frock-coat, a top hat and a long scarf to muffle his face. Father Joseph was puzzled.

"Why is the infant's godfather dressed like that?" he asked, frostily.

Without blinking, Micky said, "He caught a chill in the bottom of the sea and he hasn't been warm since."

The Merrow nodded. Father Joseph continued. The child was christened Coomara Mealiffe, and Coomara's gift to his first godchild was a lovely silver drinking beaker.

Coomara came alone to the cabin afterwards for a little celebration. He asked to hold the infant.

"Certainly," said Peggy, and handed him the small bundle.

Coomara settled by the fire. "Now let's see if my other present fits you."

He fumbled in his pocket and drew out a tiny cocked hat. He set this on the baby's head.

"Ah yes," said Coomara gently, "a nice tight fit. I'll take a glass now Mrs Mealiffe, but not poítin, if you don't mind. I don't think I've the head for it."⁹

Part Three

The Train

'Archie,' said Mr Cink, staring at me. 'That story is not in competition, don't forget.' Then he looked solemnly across at Mr Fee and said, 'I hate you for being so good.'

Mr Smyth snorted with laughter.

Thank goodness, I thought, Mr Fee wasn't in the competition. Supposing I'd felt his was the best. What would Mr Cink have said? If he didn't win he wasn't going to take it kindly. I could only hope Mr Smyth's tale was so clearly the best Mr Cink would have no choice but to bow to the inevitable.

'Where are we?' asked Mr Fee. He had noticed the train was slowing down.

I looked out the window. 'It's Athlone,' I said, recognising the signal box. We'd skirted County Meath and crossed County Westmeath. We were a third of the way to Achill already. I was surprised for a second we'd come so far. But then I'd been so mesmerized by what I was hearing was it any surprise I hadn't noticed? That was how good Mr Fee was. If I got a chance, I'd try and tell him.

The train halted beside the ladies' waiting room. There was not a porter or a passenger in sight.

'It's very empty,' said Mr Smyth.

I heard a few doors opening and a few passengers climbing out. I heard no one climbing aboard.

'It's rarely this empty,' I said. It was odd. Or was it? If hardly anyone got aboard at Broadstone, why should Athlone be any different? It was cold, mid-winter, midweek. Obviously people weren't travelling west today; they were staying home by their fires. As I had this thought, the door to the ladies' waiting room opened and I saw a half-circle of ladies with their hands held out standing around the fire inside. Then the door closed.

'You're next,' said Mr Cink, looking across at Mr Smyth.

'Why me? Why don't you go next?'

'All right, we'll toss for it,' said Mr Cink. He held up a penny. 'Heads or tails?' he demanded.

'Tails,' said Mr Smyth.

Mr Cink flipped the coin up in the air, caught it as it came down, and slapped it on to the back of his left hand.

'Tails, yes?'

'Aye,' said Mr Smyth, laconically.

Mr Cink whipped his hand away. 'Oh dear,' he said, 'heads, Mr Smyth.' He showed Mr Smyth the coin.

Mr Smyth nodded his head and muttered, 'All right, you win.'

I saw Mr Lunney, one of the guards at Athlone station walk past. He saw me and waved.

'Let's wait for everyone to get on and off, shall we?' said Mr Smyth bluntly. 'I don't want any disturbances.'

Mr Cink snorted. I heard Mr Lunney moving down the platform, closing doors. I heard Mr Lunney's whistle blowing. I heard the engine huffing and puffing. Then the train shuddered and we pulled away from Athlone station.

'"Bewitched Butter" is the name of this story,' said Mr Smyth, as the train puffed across the marshes and bogs of County Roscommon. Lough Ree lay to our right, looking like a sheet of old tin to me.

'Which butter, salted or unsalted?' quipped Mr Cink.

'No, not "Which Butter"; "Bewitched Butter".' Mr Smyth sat forward on his seat and looked up and down the compartment as if daring Mr Cink to speak. Of course, he did.

'Do you know what you remind me of?' asked Mr Cink.

Mr Smyth said nothing.

'An old pistol with the mechanism filed so fine it goes off at the slightest touch. You're a hair-trigger character – one tweak and you blow.'

The clackety-clack of the wheels filled the compartment. No one spoke. In my mind's eye I saw the door of a public house on a hot summer's evening. I glanced in. I saw men standing at the marble-topped bar, glasses of porter in their hands. The men were all jawing and guffawing, and

89

the loudest – his face red and his bowler hat pushed back from his steaming forehead – was Mr Cink. That was where he belonged, I felt, in a bar, shouting, joking, telling everyone what to do. I also sensed he belonged somewhere else, but I wasn't certain where.

'"Bewitched Butter",' Mr Smyth intoned. '"*Be*witched Butter".'

I felt a shiver run down my back and I sat up straighter.

'I'm glad to see I've already made an impression on our young listener,' said Mr Smyth, bowing slightly in my direction.

'If you think you can charm your way to a win, you're very much mistaken,' said Mr Cink, tartly. 'You're not easily charmed, are you, Archie?'

'No, sir.'

'You understand you are to pick the best story, disregarding flattery, bribery and all other seductions.'

'Yes, sir.'

'Don't they call coffee at this time?' said Mr Fee, pulling a fob out of his pocket, releasing the lid and staring at the clock face. 'Shouldn't you be at work, Archie?'

'My dear Mr Fee,' said Mr Cink, 'yes, you're right, they usually call coffee about this hour. However, what's-his-name in the galley . . .'

'Mr Cribben,' I said.

'Mr Cribben, thank you, has been paid a large sum of money, in return for which, Archie is ours for the whole journey. Didn't I explain? Silly me. The train could be packed to the gills – Archie wouldn't have to do any work. He's ours. Got it? Now, as it happens, the train's empty; there is *no* work for this young man. He'd just be sitting around idling if he weren't here.' Mr Cink paused. 'Actually, now I come to think of it, why did I pay to have him if he wouldn't be doing anything anyway? Archie, do you think Mr Cribben'd give me my money back?'

Mr Fee closed his watch. 'Let's get on with it,' he said. 'I want to hear what this stout fellow Mr Smyth has to offer.'

Mr Smyth put his small neat clenched right hand in front of his mouth and coughed. My mother and Mr Rowley, my teacher at Connor Street National School, both said to cover the mouth like that if I coughed; that's the only way I'd get anywhere, they said; '"Manners maketh man," remember that, Archie.'

I looked at Mr Smyth. I thought, he must be one of the quality. I could not imagine him standing at a bar with a mob of cronies like Mr Cink.

Mr Smyth took his hand away. He sat opposite Mr Cink with his back to the engine. His boots were highly polished with a few spots of dried mud stuck to them. He was a small, neat figure; his legs were crossed and his hands nestled, one on top of the other.

'Once upon a time, not long after Christianity came to this island,' Mr Smyth began, 'a group of monks built a town in the middle of Ireland. They built it out of hard, grey granite stone, and in no time at all it became a place men came to learn and to prepare for the priesthood; they came from all over Ireland, England and Europe. This town, which I shall call R— in my story, was a beacon shining brightly in the darkness of the dark ages.

'But then – you all know our history – our monasteries were demolished and the stone carted away to make new houses; the monks were driven across the sea; all their knowledge and wisdom and learning was lost.'

'I thought this was a storytelling competition,' muttered Mr Cink, 'not a history lesson.'

Mr Smyth ignored the interruption.

'With no churchmen to keep the place looking nice and tidy, it wasn't long before the once great town of R— became a decrepit, dusty, dishevelled village . . .'

'Steady with those Ds,' muttered Mr Cink.

'But in the countryside around this town it was a different story. In fact, without the countryside, it is likely that R— would have completely disappeared.

'The earth here was magnificently rich. It was a dark, dark black in colour but its texture was light and grainy. If you picked up a handful and worked it between your fingers, it didn't stick to you like clay; it crumbled and trickled away.'

Mr Smyth was a farmer or maybe a small landlord, I thought. He had to be. They were the only ones who talked like this.

'The grass that grew out of this earth,' Mr Smyth continued, 'was dark and rich and vividly green. So much so, indeed, that at night, even if there was no moon, the grass glowed green in the darkness.

'Travellers who passed through the area never failed to comment on this remarkable phenomenon. Nowhere else in the world except in the countryside around the town of R—, was anything like this ever seen or reported.

'With grass this powerful, cattle flourished; and from the cattle the farmers got milk; and from the milk, they made butter and buttermilk and cream and cheese and whey and anything and everything that could be made from milk.'

'Wake me when we start the story,' said Mr Cink, rudely. He deliberately gazed out the window. We were in a landscape of small smooth round hills. 'Pretty country-side,' he added, vaguely.

Mr Smyth looked at me and shook his head. I smiled back at him openly. I only did this because with Mr Cink being turned away I knew he wouldn't see. 'Bewitched Butter . . .' what could that mean? This story looked as if it could be as good as Mr Fee's.

Part Four

Bewitched Butter

'Now,' said Mr Smyth, 'we need to go back more than a hundred and thirty years to the reign of King George III . . .

'At this time one of the most prosperous farmers in the area outside R— was a man called Jeremiah O'Dwyer, affectionately known as Big O'Dwyer.

As the nickname suggests, he was a long tall man with big bones. His hair was prematurely grey and curly and his cheeks were red. When strangers met him for the first time and looked into his red-cheeked face crowned with his mop of curly hair, they always had the same thought – cherub.

But once you talked to him you found Jeremiah was nothing like a cherub. He wasn't mischievous or playful. On the contrary, he was a quiet, steady, sober fellow. He never talked about his hunting or his luck at the card table. He had a very quiet voice, as well. Have you noticed how often big fellows have quiet voices? He was modest.

He did not ride a thoroughbred horse or wear expensive clothes. He lived in a small tidy house with his wife, Maud, who was partial to a good frock and modest earrings incidentally, but was just as nice and just as neat as he was; and also in the house lived their four nice tidy children, George, Horace, Thaddeus and Louisa. Jeremiah's cowhouse was swept twice a day after each milking, and the walls were whitewashed twice a year, and his cowyard was always spotless. One visitor compared the clean cobblestones to wet plums. When ever he took his wife out in the carriage, Jeremiah always had his herdsmen wash the mud off the wheels and polish the door handles beforehand.

Jeremiah lived about ten miles out of R—, in the townland of Manor Gore. He worshipped at Ardboy, in a lovely church with a pretty square tower. Jeremiah's father, old Seamus O'Dwyer, had converted to the Protestant religion, although the rest of the clan had not. Jeremiah was uncommonly close to his relatives who still worshipped in the little Catholic chapel at Tullymargie. Jeremiah was a man with nice broad tastes, you see. He made room for everyone. If he could be criticized on any account, it was that he made too much room, too many allowances, he was a touch too easy-going.

Anyhow, life went along swimmingly for Jeremiah. His sweet-tempered cows chewed the rich dark grass. Morning and afternoon, Myles Marum, the herdsman, milked them in the cowhouse. Then, the dairyman, Francis

Marum, brother of Myles, churned the milk into butter. The butter went to the buttermarket in R— and from there it went up the post road through Borris-in-Ossory, Pike of Rush Hall, Ballydavis, Ballybrittas, Johnstown, Kill, Rathcoole, Saggart, Kilmainham, until finally it reached the great city of Dublin. Jeremiah's butter was so well liked in our capital, the wives of three earls, two members of Parliament and a bishop took several pounds every week by arrangement with Dempsey's Grocery shop near Mountjoy square . . . '

'You know Dempsey's, you must be a Dubliner then!' interrupted Mr Cink. He sounded half-astonished. 'And I had you down as a country bumpkin.'

'What?' said Mr Smyth, annoyed. We were just pulling into Kiltoom station. Between Athlone and Achill there were nearly two dozen little stations where the train stopped, and this was the first of them.

'It's an easy mistake to make. You sound so, well, rustic,' continued Mr Cink. He said this mildly but there was no mistaking the nastiness behind his words.

I heard Fee murmur, 'Oh dear.' He touched his temple with a finger and glanced around.

A whistle went. We had just arrived at Kiltoom and already we were pulling away. No one had either got on or off.

'I am Dublin-born,' said Mr Smyth coldly. 'And for your further information, I'm currently an agent for a landlord in the west, and a largish tenant farmer myself.'

Mr Smyth swivelled his small neat head one way and then the other way, his glare sweeping across the compartment like a lighthouse light. His large round eyes were blue the last time I noticed them; now they were greeny-grey, the colour of a cold, glassy sea.

'And now, no more questions, or interruptions, please,' concluded Mr Smyth.

My thoughts, entirely. Mr Cink's interruptions had unsettled the speaker and broken the spell created by the start of the story. Although it sounds an extreme thing to say, it was almost painful being dragged from the imaginary world back into the real world. It was like going out of a warm room into a cold street.

'It was a May morning, in the year seventeen hundred and sixty-four,' said Mr Smyth, 'sunny, warm and still. Myles Marum fetched the herd and drove them down the avenue towards the yard. Jeremiah always milked in the cowhouse, never the fields, although that was the practise in those bygone days, because there was less likelihood of spilt milk that way.

Swallows swooped through the air. The crows in the huge beech tree at the front of the house cackled and cawed. Myles drove the herd through the gate and into the yard, then turned back and closed the gates. The herd waited, their udders heavy with milk, their tails swishing at the swarms of bluebottles buzzing in the warm air.

The herdsman selected six beasts and drove them into the byre to start milking. This left nineteen behind in the yard. He had other animals, of course, but they had calves . . .'

'God save me from agricultural detail,' muttered Mr Cink.

That was it. I'd had enough. 'I don't mind,' I said. 'I like the detail. They make me believe Mr Smyth knows everything about the people in his story.'

'You are nauseating,' said Mr Cink, 'did you know that?' He spoke with a surprising lack of hostility. Because I'd just blurted out what I thought, there was no weakness on which to pick, and therefore nothing he could be nasty about. That was a lesson worth learning . . .

'Thank you, Archie.' This was Mr Smyth to me. He was obviously pleased I had said this.

'The back door from the kitchen opened,' Mr Smyth continued, 'and Jeremiah came out in his yard. He had eaten two sweet pieces of bacon for breakfast and there were pearls of meat caught in the gaps between his teeth. In his hand he held an ivory tooth pick with a sharp point.

Jeremiah took half a dozen steps and stopped. He pushed the end of the toothpick between a gap and freed a pearl of bacon. He spat the meat on the ground. A yard cat darted forward, picked it up with her sharp white teeth and swallowed it.

Jeremiah surveyed the waiting cows. Then he looked across at his dairy. It was by the north wall of the farm-house; a slated building, shaded in summer by a copper beech and served by running water that came in on a chute from the stream. Jeremiah could hear Francis Marum scrubbing something inside.

It was Francis who churned the milk into butter and cut it into blocks and stamped the blocks *Jeremiah's Best Butter*, then wrapped the blocks in muslin and boxed them up, ready to be carted away to the Buttermarket.

For a moment Jeremiah, with his mind's eye, saw his butter going one way to Dublin, then the guineas coming back and floating into his outstretched palm.

From the cowhouse came the chink of chain followed by a slow plaintive moan and Jeremiah's day-dream vanished as quickly as a fish vanishes when it hears a booted foot on the bank side. What a lovely combination of cowhouse sounds, he thought.

Jeremiah walked across his clean cobbled yard. He felt wealthy, prosperous, happy; not that he would have said this. Those who said things like this always ended up losing what they had. A man could only be said to be proud, if he said proud things. And he had never boasted or preened, had he? He wouldn't have wanted ever to admit this, and he never had, of course, but he was quite a marvellous fellow, really.

Jeremiah wrapped his toothpick in his handkerchief and slipped it into the pocket of his breeches. That was the moment he heard Myles shouting, "My God!" in the byre.

Jeremiah hurried in. Myles looked as if he'd washed his face in a bucket of whitewash.

"What is it?" Jeremiah asked. "What did you call out for?"

"You'd better see yourself," said Myles.

Jeremiah looked down his cowhouse. He saw six of his cows, one in each stall, each chewing a mouthful of dry yellow straw. In the stall closest to the door, there stood a red-roan Kerry cow whom they called Annie; all the cows had names, you see. The milking stool was on the floor and the milking pail was below Annie's udder. Good-tempered Annie would never kick it over.

"Look in the pail," said Myles.

Jeremiah grasped the handle and lifted up the pail. He was expecting to see a small white puddle of warm new milk that smelled of cream.

Instead, he saw a puddle with dark threads floating in it that gave off a smell of old iron. He knew this smell, he thought. It was so familiar. But where did he know it from?

He went to the door and tipped the contents of the pail into the little hollow in the top step. Now he remembered. When he had had a tooth pulled and his mouth was full of blood, that's when he'd got that smell. Those threads in the milk – they were threads of blood, weren't they?

But what could cause Annie to give blood in her milk,

he wondered? He regularly walked every inch of his grounds in search of mint, wild garlic, fool's parsley, marsh marigolds, tansy and the ox-eye daisy, all notorious causes of milk-taint. He knew none of these grew where his animals grazed, knew it as a certain fact. Well, if it wasn't anything Annie'd eaten, then that must mean she must be sick.

"What about the others?" asked Jeremiah.

"I don't know," said the herdsman.

Jeremiah fetched a new pail, and picked up the stool. He went to the second animal in the line, put the stool down, sat on it, put the pail between his knees. Then he took hold of a sausage-shaped udder and squeezed. The little hole at the end opened and a stream shot out and landed in the bucket. The milk was clean and with no blood-threads. Jeremiah tried the other four animals.

"It's only Annie," he said. He went back to her and stooped down and peered at her udder. It seemed perfectly normal. He examined the teats next, scrutinizing every inch of them. Maybe a badger had suckled her and damaged her? Although Jeremiah had never actually seen them doing it, like all countrymen he believed that badgers took milk from cows. But there wasn't a cut, a bite-mark, even a graze to be seen.

Jeremiah stood up, walked to the top of the stall and peered into Annie's face. Her eyes were not as bright as usual; there was something yellow and sticky around the rims. He looked into her mouth; the tongue, spotted with saliva and chewed up bits of yellow straw, seemed normal. Annie's nose was slightly drier than usual. He ran a hand along her flank. The bones beneath seemed to stick out a little more than he remembered. On the other hand, she was standing; she was eating. She wasn't groaning or staggering or lying on the ground.

Jeremiah said, "She doesn't seem exactly poorly."

Myles Marum nodded.

"Milk her normal. In a day or so it'll pass, I'm sure."

Myles Marum nodded again. "What do we do with her milk?"

"I'll throw it to the pig," said Jeremiah.

When the pail was full of Annie's milk, Jeremiah carried it over the yard to the end pig pen. Stella lay in the corner on a pile of old brown straw. She was due to drop a litter. The nipples along her belly stood up like a line of thimbles.

Jeremiah tipped the pail over the trough. As the milk glugged out, he saw the blood was no longer in threads running through the milk; it had got mixed up with the milk, dyeing it pink.

Stella lumbered to her feet and waddled over. She put her nose to the trough. Jeremiah heard first the exhalation then the inhalation of air as she sniffed and snorted. To his surprise, Stella turned away, waddled back to her corner and flopped down.

Jeremiah opened the door and walked out of the pen.

He was disappointed. He would go back later. Hunger would drive Stella to the trough just as milking would cure Annie.

Sadly, for Jeremiah, neither of his hopes came to pass. In fact, everything got worse. That afternoon, when he checked, he found the trough still untouched by Stella. And he found Annie had more yellow muck around her eyes and more blood in her milk. Worse still, two more animals, Hettie and Jenny, were now producing milk with bloody threads, and a couple of other animal had the tell-tale dry noses.

Jeremiah hated to see anything go to waste. He carried the tainted milk on a yoke across the yard and into the dairy.

"Make it into butter," he said to Francis, "but make certain you use one set of utensils for the good milk and another for this bloody stuff."

Two days later the butter was ready. Francis went to the door of the dairy and called, "Mr O'Dwyer!"

Jeremiah was in the cowhouse with Myles. He had just learnt that four more animals were now giving blood in their milk.

"You'd better come and see," Francis called.

Jeremiah walked over to the dairy and peered down at the butter in bottom of the churn. It appeared to have the solidity and the texture and the consistency of butter but it was the brown colour of rust.

"Dig it out, Francis," Jeremiah said. He buttered several

bits of stale bread with the rusty butter, then put all the bits of bread in the box.

"Who's them for?" asked Francis.

"The hounds."

Jeremiah left the dairy and walked to the dog-pen. Jeremiah had twelve hounds which he used for hunting both on foot and on horseback.

"Hello," he called ahead of himself, in the special tender voice he used only with his dogs. The hounds, hearing their master call, ran to the railings along the front of the pen and bayed with joy.

"Here we go then, here we go." Jeremiah called, when he got close. The hounds knew that food was coming. They yipped and yapped and cavorted with joy. Jeremiah tossed a piece of bread through the bars. A hound leapt up and caught it in mid air, then sunk on to its padded paws. Jeremiah watched. To his surprise the animal dropped the bread on the ground, whined pitifully and stepped back as if the bread was poisoned.

Jeremiah opened the gate and went in. He tumbled all the pieces of bread he still had into the feeding dish in the middle of the floor. The pack came forward, sniffed the dish and then backed away. Now Jeremiah knew he was really in trouble.

That evening, Maud found her husband at the table in the kitchen. His fowling piece, broken in parts, was scattered in front of him. He had a pole with a rag on the end and he shoved it up and down the inside of the barrel. There was a smell of gun oil.

Maud looked at Jeremiah. His face was serious; it also looked smaller. She imagined a cushion with a tear and the feathers coming out. That's how it seemed; whatever her husband was packed with inside was trickling away. What Maud saw now was the face of a troubled man who feared he was going to lose his herd, his livelihood, everything. She feared it too.

"What are you doing?" Maud asked, quietly.

"Cleaning my gun!" Jeremiah said, sharply.

Only when he was troubled did Jeremiah became impolite.

"Oh," said Maud, blithely, "and why are you cleaning your gun, now?" Although she had a pretty good idea, she thought it was better to let him tell her.

"Why do you think?" said Jeremiah.

"You're going to get us a bit of tasty woodpigeon?" she said, very sweetly. "You know how partial I am to that bird."

"No, I am not."

"Oh." She sounded completely surprised. "What *are* you doing then?"

"I'm going out to spend the night in the field with the cows. If there's something coming in, I'll kill it."

"One badger couldn't do all the harm. There'd have to be dozens at it. Besides, they'd disturb the cattle and we'd see their footprints in the grass. But we hear nothing and there are no signs in the morning."

Jeremiah said nothing.

Maud decided it was pointless to say more. He would go. Nothing would happen. He would come home in the morning. She would then suggest what she had decided they should do next and, having been out all night she fancied Jeremiah would be agreeable.

"It's cold, tonight," said Maud, kindly. "I'll boil some water for you and put it in one of the bed warmers."

"Thank you, Maud," said Jeremiah. He clicked the barrel into the stock.

Jeremiah went out after ten. He selected a tiny hummock in the corner of the field where his herd were grazing. It was May-time. There was some cloud and a small sliver of moon hung in the sky from which a little pale light leaked down on to the scene below. As usual, the grass appeared to be shining.

Jeremiah sat, the earthenware pot on his lap warming his hands, his gun beside him, the firing mechanism cocked. The cows stood and chewed, or lay on the ground and slept. He watched his herd, the ground and the hedgerow that bounded the field, the whole night through and he neither heard nor saw anything out of the ordinary.

When dawn came, Jeremiah was cold and stiff and very tired and greatly relieved.

Myles appeared. "Anything?" he asked as he approached his master.

Jeremiah shook his head and uncocked his fowling piece.

"I'll round them up and bring them in," said Myles.

Jeremiah nodded and unloaded his gun. He trudged towards the farmhouse. When he got to the yard, he decided to look at his dogs before going into the house. He went round to the pen.

"Hello, boys." The dogs bounded towards him, barking and wriggling. They were both excited and very hungry.

He peered through the bars. He saw the plate which he had left piled with bread and rust coloured butter was quite empty. It had all been eaten. That was strange. Then he realised the appalling truth; the reason he saw nothing during the night was simple; while he was out in the field, his enemy was here, gorging himself while his dogs slept.

Jeremiah found Maud in the kitchen by the fire, combing her hair. He heard the children upstairs, chasing down the corridor. He felt wretched, hopeless.

"I was coming out to you," said Maud, in her cheerful voice. "I didn't hear you firing in the night," she added.

"No, I didn't fire. I didn't see anything. Nothing came into the field." He decided to say nothing about the bread and butter which had vanished from the dog pen.

"So, no badger, nothing. And you would have seen. There was a moon."

"I suppose." He climbed on a chair and hid the gun behind the pelmet that ran along the top of the kitchen cupboard.

"You'll have to get Judy Carroll," Maud said, which was what she'd already decided was the only thing to do.

"Aye," Jeremiah agreed.

Judy Carroll was famous in R— and further afield. If an animal was sick from the evil eye or malfeasance of some sort, Judy was your woman. If she couldn't effect a cure, then no one could.

"I'll go out to see how they're milking," he said.

"No change," he said to Maud on his return. She had two eggs in a pan on the fire, spluttering and hissing as they cooked.

"It's Judy Carroll or no one," said Maud, quietly.

"Aye. I'll go now."

"Won't you have something first?"

"I'll take a piece of bread. We haven't time to wait."

While Maud buttered the bread he went to the salt hole and removed a large shining sixpence from the black bottle where he always kept a few coins.

He took the bread and his stick from the corner. "Bye," he said and went out. He had lent his horse to a neighbour and he decided it would be quicker to walk.

"Good luck," cried Maud from the doorstep.

He waved his stick and strode on.

Judy lived up in the hills, twelve miles away. Walking quickly, he thought, he would cover the distance in three hours.

The day was warm, with a lovely light wind blowing. There were big clouds moving in the blue sky. There were primroses and bluebells along the side of the road. But

Jeremiah could only think of the woman who would save his animals.

Hot and breathless, he arrived at Judy Carroll's small white cabin with its tiny windows painted blue.

"Judy Carroll!"

The door opened and Judy came out. She wore a white apron over a clean cornflower dress. She was slim, with a small bosom and very thick wiry hair that she wore in a loose bun on the back of her head. She had borne two sons, but both had died as boys, of diphtheria within days of each other. Her husband died three months later in the madhouse. It was said to be grief but it might have been drink. He was buried at Tullymargie and the night following the funeral, Mr Carroll appeared to Judy in a dream and told her how to treat sick cattle. That was ten years ago, since when she did nothing else. Judy didn't have a charge and she never discussed money. She believed that if she did she would lose her special talent. But if someone gave her money, she readily accepted it. She was usually given sixpence at the start and another sixpence once she had effected her cure. With all the sixpences she acquired, Judy lived comfortably.

"Mr O'Dwyer," she said, "your face is long."

Jeremiah walked forward and slipped the sixpence into Judy Carroll's palm. She said nothing, just closed her fingers around the coin. Then she listened while he told her the whole story.

"I'll be down this evening," Judy said, when he finished.

That evening, Judy Carroll appeared as she said she would. Sunshine slanted across the countryside. The light was very yellow. The shadows of trees and hedgerows lay dark and black across the rich green grass.

"Show me your herd," said Judy.

Jeremiah led her to the field where his animals were grazing. He opened the gate and she went in and he closed it behind.

"The sick ones have a ribbon tied round their neck," he explained. "Myles did that so you could tell them apart from the others."

"Very good," said Judy.

Jeremiah indicated the nearest animal with a ribbon. It was Annie as it happened. Judy began to walk towards her. Annie looked up and stared at Judy as she approached but she did not back away. Why didn't Annie back off? Jeremiah wondered. Cows were always nervous with a stranger.

Judy got right up, put out her hand and began to stroke Annie on her flat hairy forehead. It could only mean the worst, he thought, if Annie allowed that. The animals were bewitched, surely.

Judy pulled a square bottle of Holy Water out of her apron pocket. He and Judy worshipped in different churches. Of course his minister disapproved of Holy Water except for baptism but to Jeremiah all that mattered now was that his herd got better.

Judy sprinkled drops of Holy Water on to Annie. Then she circled Annie seven times in a clockwise direction while saying the rosary. Finally, Judy knelt on the ground in front of Annie, and while the cow looked at her, Judy stared back into her eyes and prayed. All the affected animals got the same treatment.

Jeremiah went to his bed that night feeling cheerful. His cows were cured, surely.

But they weren't. So Judy came back. She said more prayers. She sprinkled more Holy Water. She performed rites with old sixpences from the reign of Queen Anne, and special salt that came all the way from Essex, in England. But Judy's cure had no effect whatsoever. Finally, the day came when the whole herd was giving blood in their milk, and Judy, weeping gently, told Jeremiah she couldn't help him and went home.

But the herd had to go on being milked, of course. Myles and Francis tipped the milk in various places – the ash pit, the privy and the drainage ditches around the house. However, now there being so much liquid, somewhere bigger and better was needed.

"Dig a trench," Jeremiah instructed Francis, who, having no milk to churn, had plenty of time on his hands.

Francis dug a trench thirty foot long and lined the bottom with stones.

"Good," said Jeremiah, when the task was done. "Your job from now on is to bring the blood milk here and tip it."

"Aye," Francis agreed.

So Francis tipped the milk into the trench. At first it soaked away through the stones and vanished. That was that problem solved at least, thought Jeremiah grimly. Then it stopped soaking away and began rising towards the surface. Then, on the twelfth or thirteenth morning of this nightmare, Francis noticed that the earth sides of the trench, which previously had been black, had turned blood red from the milk. He showed Jeremiah.

"If things don't get better soon," said Jeremiah grimly, "we're ruined. The bad milk will poison the land." Jeremiah left the trench and went home. He found Maud at the table rolling pastry with a pin.

"We're going to be drowned in blood milk," he said desperately.

Maud stopped and looked up.

"The trench Francis dug for the milk, it's not draining. I should slaughter the herd ... sell the meat ... get enough money for a couple of new milking cows ... start again."

Maud was appalled. Slaughter the herd? Jeremiah would fall into despair if he did that. So might she. And then how long would it take him to rebuild? A lifetime, maybe.

"Listen, don't do that. Not yet. I beg you. Just wait. The animals may get better. You may spy out the reason for all of this in a day or two. Besides, slaughter the lot and you'll be destroying yourself."

Jeremiah had dreaded doing it, and therefore he was relieved to hear what she advised. "All right," he agreed quickly.

The next day Jeremiah went to Maud again after milking.

"I've been thinking, I'm going to kill one animal."

"Why?" asked Maud.

"I'll take the oldest one. If she was milking, she'd be giving the least milk and I'd slaughter her in the autumn anyway, so what odds I do it a few months earlier?"

This sounded reasonable but Maud said nothing.

Jeremiah continued, "I'll pay the Marum brothers in fresh meat this week. I'll smoke the rest of the meat and I'll pay them with smoked meat through the summer."

Maud nodded. There was good sense in this.

"I don't want to let the Marums go. When this is finished, we'll need them."

Maud nodded agreement again.

Jeremiah sharpened the butchering knives on a whetstone. Myles and Francis erected the tripod in the yard from which the carcass would be hung to be cut up and lit the fire in the smoke house. It was a Saturday; there was no school. Maud gathered the children up and herded them into the front parlour.

"You'll stay here until I come and let you out," Maud said.

She closed the shutters and slotted the drop-bar in place and locked it.

116

"But we want to see," the children shouted. "We never see."

Maud saw a pig stuck when she was a child and never forgot it. When she became a mother, she made it a firm principle that her own children would not see slaughtering done until they were sixteen.

"You're not old enough yet," said Maud. "You'll just have to wait."

She left the room and locked the door behind.

"I'll be back in an hour," she called through the wood.

"Oh please, please," the children shouted back from inside the parlour.

"No," she said.

Francis selected the oldest animal and brought her to the yard. Jeremiah fetched the butchering knives from the kitchen. Myles tied the animal to the wall and put a cut-down barrel under her neck to catch her blood. The cow began to moan. She knew what was coming. Animals always did.

"There, there," said Jeremiah, stroking a soft furry ear.

The Marums came up from behind. Francis took hold of the beast's head and bent it back. Myles ran the blade from one ear to the other. The black furry hide sprung open and flesh showed suddenly. Blood gushed out, splattering the cobbles and gushing into the half-barrel.

After a moment or two the animal heaved, like a piece of rope being given a good shake, and her legs began to buckle. Jeremiah felt relief more than sadness. He didn't like to kill an animal that had faithfully served him, but at least this way there would be meat for the Marums and his family for a month or maybe longer.

"Oh no, Mr O'Dwyer," he heard Myles murmur.

"What is it?" Jeremiah said. He didn't like Myles's tone.

The beast keeled sideways and flopped on to the cobbles.

"Lookee here." With the point of his blade Myles opened the gash wide and Jeremiah saw what he had seen. The flesh was as black as tar, and it stank too.

"That can't be eaten," said Jeremiah. It was rotten. His herd were literally rotting on their feet. He was staring disaster in the face.

The three men put the carcass on a dogcart, wheeled it off to the bog and dumped it into an old trench where there was no turf left to cut. Then Jeremiah hurried home.

He found Maud sewing a button on to a shirt.

"The meat on this cow we killed, it was filthy black and I suppose all the other animals are the same."

He stamped out. He didn't say where he was going or what he was going to do but Maud had a pretty good idea. Jeremiah had taken to spending all his time with the herd in the field, sometimes stroking them, sometimes whispering to them, sometimes simply watching them. He imagined this would help them to recover, or else let him discover the cause of their and his misfortune.

After Jeremiah left, Maud released the children; then she went back to her sewing. She felt a sense of dread. What would they do if the herd did not recover?

"Ouch!" She felt a stab of pain in her finger. A tiny blob of blood welled up out of the hole, and trembled like a jelly. In the past, when she cut herself, Maud sucked the wound clean, but today the idea disgusted her.

She wrapped a bit of rag around her finger end. She put her sewing away. She carried a chair out into the little garden at the front of the house, set the chair against the wall and sat down. The sun was shining and the stone at her back was warm.

She looked past her gate and along their lane. There were chestnut trees on either side and the leaves glistened where the light struck them. If they got no more milk they were doomed. They would lose the house, the land, everything. Everything. For a while they could live off their savings but those wouldn't last for ever. They would either end up living in a ditch, or in the dreaded Pauper House in R—, where the Indigent Society cared for the poor.

Maud trembled. The idea of the Pauper House terrified her. Men, women and children were separated when they went in. It would drive her mad. She closed her eyes and whispered, "Please don't let me go there. I don't want to lose my husband or my children. Please help me . . ."

She continued mouthing these words for several minutes. As she repeated them she grew calmer. It was a lovely, delicious feeling, just like when her mother read to her as a child, or in church, although it was only once or twice a year that prayer would have this soothing effect.

Maud opened her eyes again, and she saw the world was the same as when she last looked, except for a figure at the end of the lane. It walked through the gateway and began to stalk up the avenue towards her. It was a very old bent woman in a long black filthy skirt that trailed on the ground. Maud had never seen her before.

"Woman of the house?" the figure called.

"Yes," said Maud.

"May I step forward into your garden?"

"Yes, come in," replied Maud.

As well as the filthy skirt, she had on a little red woollen jacket, and a blouse underneath. Maud could not tell if she was barefoot or shod in boots. Her hair was grey and hung down over her ears and the back of her neck. Her face, Maud saw, when the woman came closer, was incredibly lined.

"Good evening, woman of the house."

Maud stood. She saw the woman's eyes were extremely bloodshot around the edges, and she saw that on the back of her head the woman wore a tiny and extremely grubby linen skullcap.

There was a long pause.

"It's a fine-looking house you have," the old woman said finally.

"Thank you," said Maud.

"It'll be yours, I'll fancy."

Maud was uncertain where the conversation was leading.

"Oh, I think so," the old woman affirmed. "You're O'Dwyer, aren't you?"

"I am, yes, though how you know I don't know; I have never seen or met you before."

"Oh, I know," said the old woman mysteriously. "You were Wilson before you married," she added.

"You're not from this parish, are you?"

"No," the old woman said firmly.

"Where then?"

"Oh . . . around," the old woman said, then she added quickly, "I'm thirsty you know."

Sly old bird, thought Maud. "I can't offer you much," she said.

"You've cows, haven't you?"

"We have, but I can only offer you water."

"Water," exclaimed the old woman.

"Water."

"It's a sup of milk, I need."

"You could walk to the next farm along the road. That's Phelim Brady's place. He'll give you milk."

"Why won't you?"

"We only have water."

"Water will do then."

Maud pointed towards the door. The old woman shuffled inside.

"Go down to the end of the corridor; that's the kitchen," said Maud.

When she got to the kitchen, the old woman stared

121

carefully into every corner of the room, then gazed intently into the food press, the door of which hung open, while Maud, for her part, stared at the old woman.

At first Maud was alarmed, but the old woman's naked curiosity was also strangely disarming, even comforting. The old woman was so busy poking her nose where it didn't belong, she was incapable of plotting mischief, let alone carrying it out. In Maud's experience, those who did harm were never so open about their interests.

"Lovely neat tidy shelves you have," said the old woman, finally.

Maud went out to the scullery, ladled water from the pail into a horn beaker and came back.

"Water," she said.

"You've no milk," said the old woman, taking the beaker, then drinking a sip.

Maud shook her head.

"There's a smell." The old woman sniffed the air. "Fee, fie, foe, fum, I smell blood," she whispered.

Maud said nothing.

"Would you be the wife of the man I saw in the field as I came down the avenue?" she asked quickly, "the one with his head in his hands surrounded by some of the most miserable looking cows I ever saw?"

"Probably."

Maud was aware of the old woman looking at her. Her eyes were like two small dark pebbles, each lying at the bottom of a well of wrinkled skin.

"Probably?" repeated the old woman.

Why had she said this? Of course it was Jeremiah. Who else? She felt as if she had been caught telling a lie.

"Yes that's Jeremiah O'Dwyer, my husband," she said decisively, "that you saw."

The old woman took a sip of water. "The water is nice, but you know I really want a drop of milk."

She offered the unfinished beaker back to Maud.

"That's all we have," said Maud wondering at her insistence. Then she decided to tell her the whole sorry story.

The old woman listened in silence, then went and sat down by the fire and stared into the flames for a few moments.

"Let me see this milk," she said.

Maud went over to cowhouse. Myles gave her a pail of bloody milk.

"Here," she said to the old woman as she returned and set the pail on the table.

The old woman got up and came over. She looked down. The milk in the bottom was a dark pink, as if blackberries or redcurrants had been mashed up in it. It stank of iron. Maud thought she would be sick and backed away.

"Oh, you've got trouble." The old woman screwed up her face. "I must see your husband."

Maud went to the door and called across to the cowhouse, "Myles, run down and fetch Mr O'Dwyer. Tell him there's someone here to see him."

* * *

Ten minutes later, Jeremiah came into the kitchen. He saw the old woman and looked at his wife as if to say, who's she?

"Good day, neighbour," the old woman said. "Something ails your animals."

"I suppose," said Jeremiah. He was suspicious of this stranger. Why should she consider his misfortune to be part of her business?

"Why haven't you thought to cure the creatures?" the old woman asked.

"Cure them!" exclaimed Jeremiah. "I've had Judy Carroll out for days. She did everything and anything. All pointless . . ." His voice trailed off.

"What would you do if I do it for you?"

"Do what?"

"The cure."

"Anything in our power," said Jeremiah and Maud together.

"Well, I want a silver sixpence," said the old woman, "and you must agree to do what I say."

"Surely, you'll want more than sixpence, I would think. A guinea perhaps. Or two, three, ten," Maud added, wildly.

The old woman waved her hand in the air. "Not at all. Sixpence, that's all," she said, firmly. "A silver sixpence and you do what I say. Really, I don't want any of your money, but I can't do anything unless I handle a piece of silver that comes from you."

Jeremiah got sixpence from his bottle and handed it to the old woman. She dropped the sixpence into her right boot, then wiggled her foot until she had it stowed to her satisfaction.

"Who was the man I saw earlier?" she asked.

"Myles Marum."

"Send him away and anyone else who's here or the cure won't work."

Jeremiah found the two Marum brothers and sent them home. Jeremiah returned. The old woman took off her filthy skullcap. Threaded through its edge was a white ribbon which she pulled out and gave to him. It was clean and white as if it was fresh from the laundry.

"Go out to the field and touch one of your beasts with this ribbon. One animal mind, no more. Then drive that animal back here to the yard, but make certain you don't say a word to anyone you meet on the way, going or coming, whether stranger or friend, and whether they speak to you or not. You must also not let that ribbon touch the ground. Everything will be ruined if it does, and you'll be finished, for ever. So remember, don't drop it and don't talk."

Jeremiah went off. Maud and the old woman sat down at the table to wait. Neither spoke. Maud could hear her children squealing in the nursery. They were playing Blind Man's Buff.

From the far side of the yard came the sound of the gate scraping open. The old woman and Maud got up and

125

went out the back door. From the top step they saw Jeremiah was in the yard and that the animal he had driven down from the pasture was Annie.

The old woman went up to Annie. The cow just stood stock still. She was obviously ailing, even dying, thought Jeremiah.

The old woman lifted the cow's tail. It was like a long brown rope with a furry end like the head of thistle. Still the animal made no move.

The old woman began to chant wildly to herself. She did this in Irish, not English, so neither Jeremiah nor Maud had the slightest idea what she was saying.

After some moments, and while continuing to chant, the old woman plucked a hair out of the end of Annie's tail. The cow shivered and lifted a foot in protest but was too exhausted to do any more.

The old woman repeated the process until she held in her hand nine thick red hairs that stood up like strands of copper.

The old woman stopped chanting. 'I want you to get me cream from every animal. A good lot of it. We have to churn some butter.'

Jeremiah opened his mouth, remembered what she had said to him earlier about not speaking to anyone, and closed his mouth again.

He went to the trench, filled a bucket and came back.

The old woman looked into the pail and pronounced herself pleased.

"Now fetch a churn," she said.

He fetched the old churn, the one Francis used to make the butter the hounds wouldn't touch.

The old woman filled the churn with the filthy cream and shut the lid.

"It's time to start," she announced. "No talking, just do what I say. Go to your children, Maud. Lock them up."

Maud went to the nursery, and before anyone could say a word, she had closed the door on her children inside and turned the key in the lock.

"Is it slaughtering time again?" shouted Thaddeus through the wood.

Maud banged on the door as if saying yes, then hurried away.

'Close the door, close the window and the shutters,' said the old woman when Maud returned to the kitchen. "The only light we can have is the light of the fire. And close the door to the pantry and the door to the hall, too."

Once the doors were closed, the old woman said, "You will now do exactly as I say. You will churn, you will make butter; but you will still not talk until I say you can. It won't be easy. You'll want to speak. But you can't. You mustn't. You must do this my way, and I promise we'll find out who is robbing you."

Jeremiah and Maud began to agitate the handle. A smell of iron and rust rose from the wooden box. The handle went more and more slowly as the butter began to form.

Meanwhile the old woman went to the fire and, as Jeremiah and Maud agitated the handle, she began to chant the same wild incantation she had already delivered out in the yard. Then she threw one of the cow's tail hairs into the fire.

From outside there came the horrible cry of a woman in distress. The sounds grew louder as whoever was making them drew closer and closer to the door which opened from the kitchen on to the yard.

The old woman stopped chanting, smiled and stood up.

"Open the door, we have her," she told Jeremiah, "but say nothing."

Jeremiah turned the key and pulled the door back. The old woman rushed out; Jeremiah and Maud went after her.

Outside they saw nothing; just Annie, tied to the wall, the outbuildings, the gate. From the direction of the avenue came the same horrible cries they had heard just a few seconds before but this time they were receding.

"There's something wrong," said the old woman grumpily. "Something's skewing the charm."

The old woman began to gaze about with a cross expression on her face. Suddenly she smiled. "That's it," she exclaimed, clapping her hands. "There's what's done it."

She pointed at an old horseshoe. It was nailed to the lintel over the back door, and it was so worn by weather,

128

it was virtually indistinguishable from the stone behind.

"Get that down and we'll have another go."

Jeremiah fetched a short ladder and a hammer with a claw. He climbed up and began to wrench out the nails that held the lucky charm in place. Maud stood below, holding her apron out. Jeremiah threw the nails down.

"That was the obstacle, you know," the old woman said. "My charm brought her here to the house. But she couldn't come in through the door because of that. My goodness, if we'd got her in the kitchen, we'd have had her then."

The last nail was out and the horseshoe came away. Jeremiah dropped it down. It clinked as it hit the nails in Maud's apron.

"Bring it in now, we'll try again. Put the shoe in the fire, the nails too."

Maud obeyed. Time passed. The clock chimed in the front hall. The horseshoe became red hot.

"Take out the shoe and put it under the churn," the old woman ordered.

Jeremiah picked the horseshoe out of the embers with the tongs and set it on the flagged floor. Then he manoeuvred the churn over it. The churn was on legs so there was no contact between it and the shoe and therefore no danger it would catch fire.

"We do again what we did before," the old woman said.

Jeremiah and Maud agitated the plunger in the churn, while the old woman sat at the fire, moaning, keening, and throwing one cow hair after another into the flames.

When the ninth hair was cast, the same screeching they'd heard before started up again. It was very far away.

"Hooray, she's coming, the one who did you down," shouted the old woman, apparently as unmoved by the cries as Jeremiah and his wife were disturbed by them.

The seconds slipped by. The screeching drew closer and closer. At last, whom or what ever was the cause of the racket was standing in the yard immediately outside the door.

"Go out and give her what she wants," said the old woman, "but whatever you do, say nothing – not a word. Understand? Leave the rest to me."

There was a particularly nasty cry outside.

Jeremiah went to the door and stopped.

"You have to go out. It's part of the cure."

Jeremiah opened the door and stepped out. He was greatly surprised by what he saw. It was his neighbour, Lizzie McGovern. She was standing a few feet away.

Lizzie waved her arms around and jumped about on the spot. "You must come," she shouted, "you must come."

First the screeching (which he presumed had been Lizzie approaching) and now this (Lizzie shouting). It didn't make sense. The Lizzie he knew was calm and chaste, quiet and modest. Yet the woman in front of him was most certainly her for she had Lizzie's wide freckled face, her high keenly penetrating voice, and her broad, plump body.

Jeremiah thought, one of her children is dying? Her house is on fire?

He was on the verge of shouting, "What is it?" when he remembered he must say nothing. So he went forward towards Lizzie. He tilted his head the side as if to say, speak . . . tell me the matter . . . I'll help you . . .

"My prize milking cow," Lizzie shrieked.

In a torrent of words she explained that her best animal had fallen into a deep trench in Davitt's bog. If the cow wasn't got out of the water soon, she would drown.

Jeremiah nodded to indicate that he would help. He fetched a length of rope and followed Lizzie down the avenue and up the post road. Turning into the bog, the lowing of a cow sounded in the distance. Speeding after Lizzie across the soft, boggy ground, the awful noise got louder and louder.

At last Jeremiah found himself on the upper bank of a trench. He saw the unfortunate cow bobbing at his feet. Her head was wet, her eyes were wide and her huge pale pink mouth was open as she moaned and bellowed.

The bank on the far side was at least six feet lower than the one on which he stood. Jeremiah launched himself forward and landed in the middle of a springy clump of heather.

He spun round to face the direction in which he had just come. Jeremiah tied one end of the rope to a small crooked rowan that grew a few feet away; then he made a special kind of noose at the other end of the rope; this noose would tighten but only so far.

The trouble with an animal in a bog-hole is it doesn't know you want to help it. It took Jeremiah half a dozen attempts before he got the noose over the cow's head.

Having been quiet and watchful from her place on the other, higher bank, Lizzie now shouted, "Come on, Mister, hurry it up! If you don't get my prize milking cow out of this here bog-hole, she'll die and I won't have no milk and my children will go hungry."

Jeremiah wanted to tell her to be quiet but instead he bit his lip and yanked the animal forward, pulling its head up on to the bank. The cow began to thrash about even more frantically. Jeremiah pulled harder on the rope. If the cow could just get one leg up on to the bank, then she would have enough purchase to be able to scramble out with his help. Otherwise, he'd have to leave her roped up and go and get men and horses to drag her out.

He beckoned to Lizzie to come over and help. She jumped down and took the rope with him.

Jeremiah was about to say, heave, when he remembered, no talking, so he and Lizzie didn't pull together the first couple of times. But then, miraculously, they did and suddenly, a sopping hoof was on the bank side, and then there was a second hoof beside the first, and eventually the animal heaved herself out of the water and on to dry land.

"Thank you," Lizzie cried, and smacked the cow on the mouth and shouted, "You stupid creature."

Jeremiah raised a hand as if to say, it was nothing Lizzie; then he took back his rope and hurried off in the direction of home.

When he got back the old woman was by the fire. The shutters were open and the kitchen was full of light again.

"You can talk now. Tell me what happened."

"Her cow was in a bog-hole but I got her out."

The old woman nodded. "Very good," she said, and a few moments later fell asleep.

In the afternoon Myles milked his cows, as usual, and Francis tipped the bloody milk away.

In the evening the children were fed (potatoes and salt – there was no milk or butter to moisten the spuds) and sent to bed.

The old woman woke up, stretched and yawned.

"Tell me about that woman whose cow you rescued."

"Lizzie McGovern?"

"Aye, if that's her."

Jeremiah told all he knew. Lizzie had a small farm at the back of his place; a dozen acres, a bit of bog, a few cows, a couple of goats. She was a widow woman, with four children. Lizzie was in the butter business and although her operation was smaller, by far, than his own, it was not unknown for Lizzie to match him butter box for butter box at the Buttermarket. The first time this happened Jeremiah had even wondered if trickery was involved, or if some outside agency was helping Mrs McGovern. However, he said nothing as without proof he might cause bad feeling between himself and a near neighbour, a bad thing to do in the country.

Then Mr McGovern, an exciseman, was shot in the face by a poítin maker; gangrene set in and he died some weeks later. Everyone felt extremely sorry for the widow, including Jeremiah. Mr McGovern's fellow excisemen put their hands in their pockets and got up a subscription. Lizzie used the money to buy two more cows and made even more butter (though it wasn't ever quite as tasty as Jeremiah's). She made a particularly good living from its sale, relative to the number of animals she had, but Jeremiah again banished the idea from his head of trickery or witchcraft. She was a woman one didn't suspect, one didn't accuse; she was a woman one pitied. But now it was different.

"Well," said the old woman with a grim smile when Jeremiah had finished talking, "it is not enough to have found her out; now we must punish and prevent any future ill-deeds."

"What exactly would it be that you will do?" asked Maud quietly.

"I won't do anything," said the old woman.

"Oh."

"No, I don't do anything in situations like this."

"What happens then?" asked Maud.

"I advise, and if your husband does what he is told, then everything will be fine."

Maud chewed her lip. Like Jeremiah, she felt sorry for Mrs McGovern. She found it hard to imagine Lizzie as anything other than harmless. She also loathed the idea of a dispute.

"You look worried," the old woman said lightly. "There's nothing to worry about." Then she explained what Jeremiah had to do and what would most likely happen and Maud felt better.

A little before midnight, Myles and Francis came to the back door. They each had a hound on a lead and each dog was tightly muzzled to prevent it barking.

"Go then, Jeremiah," said the old woman from her place by the fire.

Jeremiah put on his hat, took his ash plant from its place in the corner and went out, closing the door behind.

It was a moist night and the moon was hidden behind a veil of light. The three men crept down the avenue and slipped into the field. Jeremiah could make out the shape of an animal standing nearby, but the rest of the herd were lost in the darkness.

They set off across the wet grass, aiming for the white blob that shimmered in the darkness more or less in the middle of the field. They took care, with each step, to make as little noise as possible.

At last they arrived. The white blob was in fact a

collection of flowering thorn bushes. On the outside there was a wall of tangled hawthorn branch, while in the middle there was an empty space where a man could comfortably stand.

Jeremiah covered his eyes with his hands and pushed backwards into the thornbush. He felt a thorn stab him on his shoulder blade, and then another thorn prick him lower down, closer to his kidney. Then there was nothing. He had arrived in the middle. Jeremiah opened his eyes. Myles and Francis appeared at his side a few seconds later. The hounds snuffled at his feet. Jeremiah wondered if this was a little like being inside a snowball. Each man took up a position looking out through the tracery of branches into the field beyond. It was too dark to see much.

Then, suddenly, the clouds parted. There was a moon in the sky; it was large though not full, and it lit up the scene below. Jeremiah could make out several cows standing close to him with their dipping backs and heavy hanging udders.

For the next while, nothing happened, other than that the night wore on. Then, close to the hedgerow on the other side of the field, Jeremiah sensed something moving.

A few moments later, he heard the shuffle of a cow stamping nervously on the ground; this was followed after a few moments by a low plaintive bellow.

Myles and Francis slipped over and stood beside him,

stock still. They held the leashes tightly so the hounds understood they, too, must remain still.

From out of the darkness, Jeremiah and the herdsmen heard the same pair of sounds repeated and repeated; first the stamping and then the bellowing. It was maddening not to know what this was.

Then, at last, Jeremiah saw something glistening in the moonlight. It was low and sleek with high ears at front and powerful legs at the rear. It was a hare, the biggest he had ever seen. It crawled along the ground in the way he imagined a serpent moved.

He watched as the long low furry shape pushed itself, nose first, through the wet grass, making scarcely any noise, until it had brought itself right in under the belly of a cow. Then in a single elegant sinuous movement, the hare stood up on its hindquarters, clasped a teat between two front paws in a way that seemed much more human than hare-like, and began to suckle from the udder. The cow shifted its feet nervously and bellowed and Jeremiah realised this was what he had been hearing every night.

The hare remained as it was, sucked at the teat for a few seconds more, then dropped down on to its front paws and skidded out from under the cow, taking care to avoid its prancing hindquarters. It ran on, slowly, its belly swollen and full of milk, before cautiously slithering towards the next animal it intended to suckle, who stood some yards off, away to Jeremiah's left.

Jeremiah raised his arm in the air, the agreed signal.

The muzzles were slipped, the leashes released. The hounds blundered blindly through the under-parts of the thornbush and burst out on the far side into the open pasture baying loudly. Jeremiah closed his eyes and charged forward. A second later he was into the open field.

The hare was on its haunches, its neck stretched horribly forward and its mouth wide open. There was something shooting from its mouth.

The hounds were speeding across the dew-wet grass. He ran forward after them. The hare turned and dashed for the most distant hedgerow.

A few seconds later, Jeremiah reached the spot from where the hare had started. He looked down and saw a puddle of sick on the grass.

The hare was now a far-off blur near the hedgerow on the other side of the field. The hounds were in-between himself and the hare. The hare with its belly empty, Jeremiah realised, was going to be far harder to catch than the hare with its belly full.

Jeremiah reached the hounds. Their noses to the ground, they were running around in agitated circles, snorting and snuffling. The hare was gone.

Francis clicked his fingers to catch the dogs' attention, and then clicked his fingers again as if to say, where's the hare?

The hounds jerked their noses this way and then that. There seemed to be no rhyme or reason to what they did.

Then they bolted through the hedgerow. A moment later, Jeremiah heard his dogs baying on the far side. They had located the scent. They were in pursuit.

The men ran down their side of the hedgerow. There was no passage so Jeremiah tore through to the track on the far side.

Jeremiah looked to his right. He could dimly perceive the outline of his dogs further down the track. He heard them as well.

The dogs vanished. Jeremiah, with Myles and Francis now behind him, ran forward. They eventually reached a short, tree-lined avenue, at the end of which stood Lizzie McGovern's cabin.

Jeremiah ran forward. He emerged from under the trees on to a flat piece of ground covered with flagstones. There were two tiny windows beside the cabin door. The shutters inside were closed over but he could see tiny threads of light around the edges. The hare and the hounds were nowhere to be seen.

Suddenly, the hare appeared around the corner of the cabin and ran along the front of the house, right in front of him. It stopped at the front door and pushed with its paws against the splash board on the bottom.

One of the hounds hurtled round the corner. The hare gave up trying to open the door, ran along the front, and disappeared around the other corner. The second hound appeared. The two dogs ran past Jeremiah in pursuit.

Grasping his ash plant, Jeremiah went the other way. If

he caught the hare between himself and the dogs, he had a good chance of hitting it. Coming out at the back, he saw the hare running towards him.

Jeremiah raised his ash plant. The hare stopped by the back door. Seconds seemed to last for minutes.

Jeremiah moved to block the animal's escape to the orchard. The dogs did the same. Myles and Francis appeared, following the path of the hounds. Lizzie's back entrance was a traditional stable door and it was closed. The hare was trapped. There was no escaping now.

Except suddenly, the hare sprung upwards and struck the top door with its head. The door began to swing away. The hare threw its paws forward, and, at the same time, scrambled desperately with its back legs against the lower door. Its body was on the edge. In a moment it would flop over and be gone. The dog closest to the cabin leapt forward. Jeremiah expected to see the hare slip over the far side of the door and vanish. But the dog launched itself forward, with its mouth open and its teeth glinting faintly, then closed its mouth savagely on the haunches of the hare. The hare screamed like a child in pain. The dog sunk back. The bloody rump of the hare slid over the top edge of the door and was gone. From inside the cabin came another awful scream.

Jeremiah ran forward and kicked the door open. In two bounds he was in the middle of Lizzie McGovern's kitchen. There was a great sheet of black-red blood on the hard earth floor. There were two candles in candle holders

140

burning on the table near the front windows. A good fire was roaring in the hearth. The four McGovern children and some older McGovern relatives were there. They stared at Jeremiah, open-mouthed.

Jeremiah saw no sign of the hare. He noticed the little door to the bedroom at the side of the hearth was open. He saw blood in the doorway and from the room heard a horrible moaning.

Jeremiah ran to the table and picked up a candle holder with a smoking candle and walked into the small bedroom. There was a bed in the corner piled with blankets. He lifted the candle and passed it one way and then the other while he stared into the dark corners. He expected to see the hare, crouching, cowed, its eyes glinting fearfully, waiting to spring, waiting to flee. But he saw nothing; just a box, a washstand, a pitcher and ewer.

Something stirred. Myles and Francis crashed into the room after him.

Jeremiah lifted his hand as if ordering them to be quiet. The hare must be under the bed, he thought. Myles and Francis stopped in their tracks. Jeremiah strained his ears.

Again, he heard the stirring. It was coming from under the covers.

Jeremiah pointed at the blankets.

Myles took the end of the covers and jerked them away. At first Jeremiah didn't know what he was looking at. Then he brought the candle forward. He saw the back of a pair of legs, the flesh torn, as if by teeth, right the way

141

down their entire length; blood was gushing from the wounds and a glistening pool of red was swiftly spreading across the mattress underneath. He saw the back of an unmarked upper torso. He couldn't see the face. But he didn't need to see.

A voice cried from the door, "Mother."

The figure bleeding in the bed was Lizzie McGovern . . .

Three days later Lizzie finally died of the mauling. The parish priest in Tullymargie wouldn't let the family bury Lizzie with her husband in the graveyard beside the church. Lizzie's body had to go on other side of the graveyard wall, in unconsecrated ground. Only the children and close family relatives attended the funeral. The priest would not officiate but sent the young curate in his place.

The old woman stayed on with the O'Dwyers. She spent her days dozing by the fire or eating (her appetite was enormous), and her nights wandering around the countryside. Before the month of July had ended, the cows were giving gloriously rich summer milk. Francis started churning again and it wasn't long before Jeremiah's best butter was travelling up the road to Dublin again, and money was flowing back in the opposite direction.

Early one morning, at the start of August, the old woman announced her intention to leave.

"Why not stay here? We'll look after you," said Maud. "You never have to leave." The old woman had saved them from poverty. Maud was happy to take the woman in and feed her, and bury her properly when her days ended.

"No, I'm done here," the old woman said.

She left that afternoon. She promised to return but Jeremiah and Maud knew in their hearts they would never see her again.

A couple of nights later, some men from R— got wind of the unusual funeral that had taken place and why. The men got drunk, stumbled through the darkness to the McGovern cabin and pegged stones through the windows.

The next day, Lizzie's brother, who was staying in the house with the children, took them away to Longford and the McGoverns were never heard from or seen again, either.

Lizzie's brother tried to sell the cabin but no one would buy it. After a couple of years the thatch went green; after a couple more years, the roof timbers rotted and crashed to the ground. Local farmers hauled away the stones to make new buildings. All that remained, eventually, were a few stones that were too heavy to cart away, and the dark oblong shape of the cabin floor where Lizzie's children once played. Then briars and thorns grew up and the site was covered completely.

Time flowed on. Jeremiah and Maud died. But the story lived in memory. I visited R— as a boy. My uncle was the Rector at Ardboy. He was on good terms with the priest at

Tullymargie and that priest had a man, Roderick Mulligan, who worked in the graveyard. Roderick told me that sometimes, when he went into the graveyard very early in the morning before anyone was about, he would often find an old hare sleeping on the grave of a long dead exciseman, name of McGovern. At the sound of Roderick's boots crunching on the gravel path, the hare would jump over the wall and disappear, but after a day or two, it always came back. '

Part Five

The Train

I was in a dream. When my imagination is fired up, the real world fades and the pretend world is everything. And now it was over, it was like waking from a wonderful sleep. I felt happy and warm. I imagined Mr Fee and even Mr Cink felt the same because neither were speaking. It was like a spell had been cast over us all.

I heard the wheels rattling on the tracks. Through the window I saw small fields with stone walls and great clumps of gorse. We were just past Ballinlough. Since Kiltoom we'd stopped at half a dozen stations (I could rattle their names off by heart – Knockcroghery, Ballymurry, Roscommon, Donamon, Ballymoe and Castlerea) but today I hadn't noticed them.

Did I like 'Bewitched Butter' as much as Mr Fee's story? Both had put me into a mild trance, so they both did the work that a story must do. I couldn't say one was better than the other. What I could say for certain was both were good. But with any luck Mr Cink's would be bad and

I'd be able to award the prize without any argument to Mr Smyth.

I heard someone cough. It was Mr Fee. He said, 'Yes, I liked that. That was very well done.'

Mr Cink clapped his hands. 'My go now. Make way for the champion. No interruptions.'

Messrs Fee and Smyth ignored this boast.

'I want to move. May I?' continued Mr Cink, very sweetly. Mr Fee looked blank. 'I want to swap seats with you, Mr Fee,' he said, slowly.

'What's wrong with your seat?' asked Mr Smyth. He lit a match, then sucked the flame down into the bowl of his pipe.

'I feel like a change,' said Mr Cink in a soft voice. 'I'm tired of this window and that far corner looks so much more snug.'

Mr Smyth blew the match out. 'The reason you want to change seats, Mr Cink, is so you can sit opposite our judge, the boy here, and corrupt him.'

'Not corrupt!' exclaimed Mr Cink. 'But I admit, I want eye contact, as you and Mr Fee had when you told your tales. The teller must always see the eyes of the listener.'

Mr Smyth exhaled a gust of smoke, then took the pipe from his mouth. The stem was wet. 'Archie,' he said, rising smartly to his feet, 'stand up.' I did as he said at once. I could tell it was important.

'Right,' Mr Smyth continued, shooting past me and dropping into the corner where I'd been sitting. 'You take my seat, Archie, and Mr Cink here will tell you his story.'

I sat down in Mr Smyth's old seat with my back to the engine. Mr Cink, I saw, was scowling slightly. Why? I was puzzled. He'd got his eye contact, hadn't he? He'd be able to stare straight at me. Then I realised. Mr Cink had wanted to be the one to move but Mr Smyth had out-manoeuvred him. Clever Mr Smyth.

What a treat the day was turning out to be. I was sitting in a first class compartment. I had no work. All I had to do was sit and listen. A part of me was worried by Mr Cink but at least I wasn't alone. If Cink's story was clearly bad and Mr Smyth's was clearly better, I could bank on the support of Mr Fee. On the other hand, Mr Cink's tale might be the best of the day. He liked to show off; he loved the sound of his voice. Maybe, when telling a story, these character traits might make him the best storyteller of the three. But if he won he'd be insufferable.

'The name of my little tale,' began Mr Cink, 'is "Daniel O'Rourke".' As he spoke, Mr Cink stared at me.

'My tale is a combination of fantasy and adventure with a dash of whimsy, which I hope will please this little fellow before me.'

Mr Smyth snorted, and smoke billowed from his mouth. It assumed the shape of a ring, quivered for a second or two, then began to float up towards the ceiling.

'Impressive, Mr Smyth,' said Mr Cink. 'Quite the smoke-ring artist, aren't we?'

Mr Smyth said nothing.

'In my story I will conjure up real people in real situations, instead of the pretend people in pretend situations that you attempted to palm off on us. Your story has no more substance than that smoke ring, whereas mine shall be as solid and substantial as this carriage.'

Mr Smyth said, 'Is that so?' and blew another smoke ring.

'You're going to get slaughtered,' boasted Mr Cink.

He turned his gaze on me again. His thick grey hair grew out from the crown in every direction and then stopped at a line that circled his head. It was as if the barber had plonked a pudding bowl on his skull and followed the rim with his scissors.

'Young fellow,' Mr Cink asked me, 'are you familiar with the town of Bantry?'

'Umh.'

'I'm to take that as a no, am I?'

'Yes.'

'Yes it's a no, is that it? Or yes, it's a yes. Which is it, Archie?'

'Ah . . .'

'You're going to have to be quicker than that,' he said tetchily before I had a chance to reply.

'I haven't been to Bantry, sir.'

'It's a no then?'

'Yes.'

'Well, then, why didn't you say no?'

'Didn't I . . .'

'No, you said yes.'

'Oh.' My face flushed red.

'If it's no you say no, and if it's yes you say yes. It's elementary English.'

'Yes.'

'Or do you really mean no?'

'Yes . . . I mean no . . . no, I mean . . . yes.'

'You do speak English, don't you?'

'If it's a yes you say yes,' I said, 'so yes, I do.'

How I had the gumption to throw Mr Cink's words back to him, I'll never know; but I did and the other two laughed.

'Well done,' said Mr Cink. He was chuckling too, but he didn't seem to be enjoying it as much as they were. 'You're a quick wit, young Archie. Let's see if your judgement is as sharp.'

'I'm sure it is,' said Mr Smyth.

'Well, you would say that, wouldn't you. Actually, he's a nauseating goodie-goodie in whose mouth butter won't ever melt. Aren't you, Archie?'

As always, Mr Cink contrived to have the last word.

Part Six

Daniel O'Rourke

'No interruptions, please.'

Mr Cink cleared his throat.

‘Once upon a time there lived, in the town of Bantry, a man called O'Rourke, first name Daniel. Once or twice a week, I went in to town to buy provisions, to transact business, and so on . . .

Now the way I went in to Bantry was past a fairy fort called Dullaveen Court and down Misery Hill. Daniel O'Rourke lived at the bottom of Misery Hill, in a tiny place with crooked windows and a warped door. Daniel's old employer put Daniel here once he was too old to work on the estate. It was just one storey, two rooms. Daniel didn't like it. He didn't want to die in this rotten little house. He wanted to die on the estate where he had lived all his life. But this was not to be.

Old O'Rourke, as he was called locally, had a bit of a reputation. As a boy he was a celebrated hunter, always snaring rabbits and tickling salmon and robbing the nests of birds. He was a wild boy but he was marvellous attractive for all his wildness, as wild boys so often are.'

Mr Cink only said this to appeal to me.

'As he grew older, Daniel turned his attention to whiskey, as men do. He became a famously good dancer. But most importantly of all, he was also said to have spent the night with the fairies. Wouldn't it be marvellous, I thought, if it was true and that there really was another race on this island beside ourselves? I was also told that Daniel had become a good storyteller with age, especially when he told of "that night". The story connoisseur in me was intrigued.

I decided I would make friends with Daniel. Accordingly, every time I saw him sitting outside his wretched house, I'd stop and I'd say, "Good day, Mr O'Rourke," and "How are you?" Daniel and I would talk, or to be absolutely precise, he'd talk and I'd listen. He really was a gabbler and it soon became clear why Daniel had been shipped off the estate and sent here to die; he couldn't stop talking.

Anyway, over time, Daniel and I became better and better friends. Then, one summer's day, fifteen years ago, I decided I'd had enough courtship. I wanted the story, now.

"Daniel," I said. Daniel was sitting on an upturned box

leaning against the wall. "Can I ask you something?"

"Yes, Mr Cink."

"Do you mind if I sit down?"

"No, Mr Cink."

Daniel's front door step was granite, and very cold to sit on. Spend an hour on a step like that and you'd have collywobbles. Luckily, I had just bought the *Guardian*, the Bantry variety that is, a newspaper which is famously thick. I spread it on the step and sat down.

"Daniel," I said, "you have many remarkable stories, I know, but there's one story, I'm told, that's more remarkable than all the other stories put together."

"Is there your honour? I wonder which one could that be?"

"Don't be irritating, Daniel. You know exactly which one I mean. It's the moon story."

He was silent. I wondered if he was offended. It was time to take action, I produced my snuffbox, and set it beside me on the step so he could help himself.

"Thank you, your honour."

Daniel put a pinch of brown powder up each nostril. Then he sneezed twice, blowing two worms of mucus speckled brown with my snuff on to his filthy red handkerchief.

"That's better," said Daniel. For several seconds he stared intently at what had just come out of his nose, then he folded his handkerchief away and stowed it in his pocket. "Nothing like snuff to clear the head," he said.

157

A tiny fur of brown dust, I noticed, was left behind in his grey moustache. I was going to tell him he was acting like a disgusting old man but I decided not to.

He offered my snuffbox back to me. "No, Daniel, you keep it. Help yourself if you need more. Don't stint. Now get going. I haven't all day."

Daniel cleared his throat. "Well, your honour, Mr Cink," he began, "it was many years ago . . ." and this is the story Daniel told me.'

'Thank goodness, the story,' sighed Mr Smyth. 'I thought the preamble was going to last for ever.'

'You're making me angry,' said Mr Cink. 'If I hear any more from you, I shall personally throw you out the window.'

'I doubt I'd fit,' said Mr Smyth, cheerfully.

'And I wouldn't let you,' added Mr Fee.

'Just you try and stop me,' said Mr Cink. 'Now please, I pray silence for the tale of Daniel O'Rourke.'

'When he was a young man, Daniel O'Rourke worked on the estate of Derby Savage, Esquire, who lived at Reeky Hall, a few miles south of Bantry. Mr Savage had a forest where he shot pheasant and rabbit and deer; Daniel was gamekeeper and he kept the grounds nice and he kept the poachers out; he also did ditch cleaning and hedging. He was a labourer, really, who was occasionally allowed to hold a gun.

Mr Savage senior had a son, one son. He was called Henry – Henry James Wiltshire Savage. Henry went away to India at twenty-one, to join a Cavalry regiment of the East India company. After ten years, Henry married a girl in Calcutta called Leonora and came home to Reeky Hall.

Well, Mr Derby was so delighted, he decided to hold a celebration dinner for all his estate workers and tenants. Knowing his tenantry were apt to be wild when bunched together, he decided to hold the event in the schoolroom, half a mile from the hall.

The servants were set to work. Table linen was washed and starched. Delft and cutlery were fetched from the attic and dusted down. Trestle tables were repaired and erected in the schoolroom. Pheasants were hung and then plucked. Hams were dug out of the salt barrel and soaked. Salmon were caught at the weir and brought up to the hall packed in boxes of straw. Peas and cauliflower, carrots and spuds were dug up from the kitchen garden. Daniel helped with the digging.

Finally, the night of the dinner came. The food was devoured. Toasts were drunk. Mr Derby gave a silver sixpence to every person in the room, man, woman, and child. The tables were pushed aside and the musicians came in; they began to play sets, jigs and reels. Mr Derby danced with Leonora, Mr Henry's bride.

Daniel danced with Megan Meehan, a kitchen-maid up in Reeky Hall and the girl he was going to marry; she was a nice jolly female with a red face and fleshy solid arms.

Mr Derby had promised the couple a cottage in a year or two. They would not tie the knot until they were given it.

After two dances Megan Meehan said, "I'm hot." Daniel took her outside and led her under the spreading branches of an old oak tree. When she lent against the tree, Megan was worried the green dust of the bark would get on her dress.

"Don't talk rot," said Daniel, in a passable imitation of Mr Derby's fruity way of talking. He kissed Megan.

"Your mouth tastes of whiskey," Megan said afterwards.

"And yours tastes of cake," he replied.

Towards midnight, the Savage family retired to Reeky Hall. All their servants went with them, including Megan Meehan. She had to be up at five o'clock the next morning to light the stove and start the breakfasts.

With the cat away, the mice could play. Daniel danced with one girl after another, and drank one whiskey after another.

Some hours later, he found himself by the big school window. He felt light-headed and breathless, and very, very hot. All he could recall of the evening was a blur of glasses tilting, liquor flowing, and his feet pounding in a rhythm that went faster and faster . . .

Daniel mopped his face and looked through the window. There were clouds scattered about the sky. There was also a moon. It was white, like chalk, with smudges, here and there, on its smooth flat face.

What were they, he wondered? Megan often had little black soot patches on her face after she lit the kitchen stove.

He noticed what looked like the tip of a thorn, or the head of a splinter, if you like, sticking out of the left side of the moon.

"What's that!" Daniel exclaimed.

It was incredibly thin and small. This must explain why he had never seen it before. He blinked and looked again. This time the edge of the moon was perfectly true and smooth. Daniel was relieved; he liked to think there was nothing he didn't see or know . . .

The musicians struck up a polka. It was a nice bright piece like water running along a stream bed. Daniel heard laughter, feet scuffing the floorboards, the roar of the crowd. He had never known such a night; he doubted he would ever know its like again, either.

He began to feel tearful. But then suddenly, instead of hot tears on his cheeks, he felt faint and unsteady on his feet.

Daniel put his boiling forehead against the pane of glass closest to him and shut his eyes. He fancied the cold glass would draw all the heat out of him, like a poultice draws out poison from a boil. In fact, everything went cold so quickly, he thought he felt goose bumps on his brain.

He opened his eyes quickly. Beyond the glass he now saw not one but three trembling moons. He felt terrible.

A moment later, Daniel found himself in the little porch tacked on the end of the building. It was cold and there was a geranium in a pot on the windowsill. It had a chalky smell.

How had he got here?

There were candles with reflectors hanging on the wall, he noticed. He found his coat, his hat, and his stick in the corner. Then he lifted the brass latch, stepped out, and closed the door behind.

He felt the cold of the night first on his face, and then on his chest and back as his damp shirt froze. It was shocking but refreshing. He stepped along the path. The gravel was clean and hard.

But now, he wondered, what should he do? Should he go back to his little room? If he went to sleep now, he wouldn't wake up until the afternoon. Then, when evening came, he wouldn't be able to sleep. It would be days before he was back to his regular sleeping pattern.

No, he decided, he'd stay up. Of course, he'd be a bit tired later on, but that's what you paid for a wonderful night.

Daniel realised he needed something to occupy himself. He couldn't go to work. Mr Derby had given all the estate workers (though not the servants in the hall) the day off. He needed to visit someone. Megan was asleep, and everyone else he knew was whizzing up and down the floor in the schoolroom.

Then, Daniel remembered Mrs Hardigan, first name,

Hester, a sometime scullery maid at Reeky Hall. Now, eighty years old and a recluse, Mrs Hardigan lived in a little cabin outside the demesne. She was rumoured to be a witch; she certainly did cures and her speciality were swollen, inflamed or stiff joints.

In Daniel's case, it was his big toe joints that were the problem; they were permanently red, swollen and puffed up. It always hurt him horribly to pull his boots on first thing, and it always hurt to walk at the start of the day until he became accustomed to the pain. Dancing, on the other hand, was different; dancing Daniel could manage; with enough whiskey in him, he never felt his feet.

Daniel had been meaning to see Mrs Hardigan for months. So why didn't he go now? After a night on the floor, his joints would be more than usually red and inflamed, and therefore especially easy for Mrs Hardigan to see. She'd probably be asleep when he reached her cabin but he didn't doubt she'd be delighted to see him. This, of course, was the confidence of one who had had too much whiskey.

Daniel left the demesne. The country got wilder and wilder.

At last he came to the bank of the River Dunne. Mrs Hardigan lived in the townland of Aghaveigh, on the other side.

The distance from one bank to the other was a good fifty feet; the means of crossing were two dozen stones laid in a line. This place was known as Knowles's ford.

Daniel stepped on to the first stone. He continued, moving from one stone to the next, at a nice easy pace. Halfway over, he stepped on to one as big as a millstone. He stopped. All round him, water streamed past. As it bumped over stones and veered around boulders it made a bright cheerful noise. Just like a polka, he thought.

And then he noticed something silver sparkling in front of him. Was this on the surface or was this in the water, he wondered?

Daniel waited for his dull but extremely happy brain to grind out an answer.

Did stones sparkle in that way? None that he'd ever seen. Did fish? No. Never. What ever it was, it wasn't alive.

His brain slowly chugged on. Suddenly, it was obvious – blindingly so . . .

You had to give Mrs Hardigan silver before she'd do the cure; sixpence or a shilling usually. Daniel was going to give her the sixpence he had from Mr Derby earlier in the evening. Those silver sparkling shapes were surely sixpences or shillings that supplicants, like himself, had dropped in the water?

He laid down his stick, took off his coat, and pulled up his sleeve. He laid down flat on his stomach, and reached into the water. Oh, it was icy. Never mind, he thought. He closed his fingers over a bright coin, and lifted his hand out. Then he opened his fingers, all happy and excited. To his surprise he saw he was holding nothing but a fistful of grit.

He reached back into the stream and lunged at another silver coin; but all he got was another fistful of grit. He made a third attempt. Same again; grit and nothing else.

Daniel got to his feet. He could see the silver sparkles dancing everywhere. What were they?

After a pause, the answer came. It was the light of the moon, caught on the high points of the water, and then magically re-directed to the river-bed.

Daniel laughed. "Oh, Daniel O'Rourke, you'd better be careful. You mistook moonlight for money, you fool . . ." He rolled down his sleeve, put on his coat, retrieved his stick, then gazed up. He saw huge clouds with silver crowns, a black sky scattered with stars, and the moon – big, round and white.

"What a beautiful night!" Daniel said. He sighed and stepped forward. A fraction of a second later, he realised there was nothing underneath his feet.

The stick left his hand and flew one way. His hat went the other way. He was going to strike the water. Daniel could swim so drowning did not worry him. Also, the river was shallow. He must land feet first and avoid falling. Especially backwards. If his head hit the stepping-stone behind, his skull would crack like an egg.

Daniel stepped forward in the air. A moment later, he hit the water. He heard the splash he made. His feet went in first. He flexed his legs. Any moment now, he would hit the hard river-bed. He doubted the water would reach much above his knees. He hoped he wouldn't twist his ankle . . .

But what was this, thought Daniel? No river-bed beneath his feet. He was just falling, down and down and down . . .

This didn't make sense. Daniel didn't know that on the far side of the stepping-stone that he had just left, a deep fissure ran along the middle of the river-bed. Daniel was sinking down into its murky depths.

As he sank, he was not frightened but he was perplexed. Then he stopped (this was because of the air in his lungs: without air he could have sunk another fifty feet – that's how deep the fissure went) and Daniel began to rise . . .

A moment later, Daniel's head burst through the surface. He began to gulp air. At the same time, he gazed around.

He saw his stick and his hat shooting away. He had a vague impression of the stepping-stone he had wanted to reach. It was somewhere away to his right. He began to swim towards it but could make no progress; the strong current carried him downriver.

Daniel was swept on like a cork and the riverbanks rushed past him, one in shadow, the other a white blur lit by the white moon. Every now and again a little wave would slap his face and he would get a mouthful of brackish river water. Daniel was soon very tired and very cold.

Oh, woe, Daniel thought. If he couldn't get out soon, he'd freeze to death or drown. The happiness he had known a few moments before was gone. He had lost Megan, he had lost everything. He heartily wished he had never started on the journey to see Mrs Hardigan.

A few moments later, Daniel became aware that the river was widening. Like something fired from the mouth of a cannon, he shot out into Lough Dunne. Here he continued to hurtle along as quickly as before.

Daniel saw the silver edge of something sticking up in front of him, out of the water. A very large fish perhaps, or a whale? No, not on an Irish lake, he realised. No, this was an island. He might get out here, he thought, and then he might get dry.

Then, horrified, he realised the current wasn't carrying him towards the island, but around it, for that was the line followed by the fissure which cut along the bottom of the lough, several hundred feet below him.

Whizzing past the left hand side of the island, Daniel saw a tree in front of him. It was a stunted alder, and it grew, not upwards but sideways out of the island's shore, only twelve or fifteen inches above the surface of the lake.

As the current was about to carry him under the tree, Daniel reached up and grasped it. The alder bent under Daniel's weight, but it did not break. At the same time, an ominous soughing came from the direction of the roots, but they held.

Daniel worked his hands along the length of the alder. The horrible soughing grew louder and louder. At the very moment Daniel felt the soft yielding mud of the shore underfoot, the entire tree came out of the ground, roots and all. While the alder plopped into the water and was borne away by the current, Daniel scrambled out with enormous difficulty.

At last, Daniel made dry ground. Waving his arms for warmth, he began to hurry forward. The island was flat. It was all bog, he guessed. He was on a hard crust that floated, in turn, on a wet sea of peat. He didn't even know the island's name. Since he was born, twenty-six years earlier in a small cabin behind Reeky Hall, he had only visited the shores of Lough Dunne once, and he had never ventured out on her waters in a boat, ever.

He shivered and stumbled on, the ground appearing to shiver with him beneath his feet. It was like running on a vibrating drumhead that could only just take his weight. If he stopped, it would tear. But he never stopped. He was desperate to find a house; if there was a house, then there was a man; and if there was a man, then there was certainly a boat; if there was a boat, he could get away from this wretched place and go home.

But Daniel found nothing, not even a ruin. Gradually, it dawned on him that nothing and no one lived on this island.

A little way ahead, Daniel saw a small, rather ugly stone lit up by moonlight. He decided he'd sit down and have a rest. When he got his breath back, perhaps he might feel more cheerful.

Daniel sat down. His breath did indeed come back. But he felt even more sorry for himself. He was going to have to jump into hateful Lough Dunne and swim ashore, he thought. But what if the current whisked him out into the middle? It was a risk he'd have to take.

At that moment, he noticed a pale shadow floating across the boggy ground.

He looked up. His heart froze. There was something between himself and the moon. It was big, it was black and it was moving towards him.

Daniel's mouth ran dry. It was the Devil, he thought, come to take him.

He opened his mouth to say the Lord's Prayer but his tongue wouldn't move. He went to stand but his legs wouldn't move either.

He was frozen on the spot, he realised, and in a second, in less than a second, two great cold burning hands would close around his throat and squeeze. Or two great finger-nails would slip into his eye sockets and lever out his eyes. Or perhaps the Devil would twist his body and his head in different directions and the two would come apart like corn from the stalk.

"Daniel O'Rourke?" he heard.

He glanced sideways and upwards. He was terrified yet he was unable to stop himself. To his great surprise, what he saw was not the Devil but a huge feathered chest, and a head with a beak on the end. It was an eagle, gliding slowly in his direction.

"Daniel O'Rourke," the eagle continued, "how do you do?" The eagle touched down and immediately began to half-walk, half-glide in a wide circle around him. It looked ridiculous but Daniel knew perfectly well it demanded respect.

"I'm very well, thank you very much, sir. And I hope you are too." Daniel spoke with as much charm as he could muster.

Meanwhile, Daniel was of course wondering, how did an eagle come to speak like a man? Could he ask? A second later, he decided, no. In his experience, those with fierce temperaments did not like questions.

"Well, Dan," the eagle continued, still circling, still friendly, "what's brought you here?"

Was this horrible island this eagle's home, Daniel wondered? He must make it clear – although without giving offence – that he wanted to be away from here as soon as possible.

"Nothing brought me here, your honour, in the sense you mean."

"You haven't come here for any reason, you mean?"

"No, sir. You see, the fact of the matter is, I didn't mean to come here. I was crossing the river at Knowles's ford. Rather than watching where I was going, I was looking up at the moon. I stepped straight into the river and got washed down into Lough Dunne. Eventually I saw this island – which is a lovely looking place, if I may say – and I managed to get ashore. I now want to go home."

"Do you?"

"Yes, I do, sir, sincerely."

"You really want to leave this island, do you?"

"Oh yes, sir, gorgeous though she is."

"You've been drinking, haven't you?"

There was no point in lying. "Yes, sir," said Daniel.

"Do you know what I think of people who drink?"

"No, sir, I don't."

"I think they're stupid. And you, Daniel, you are very, very stupid. Which is why you stepped into the river."

"Yes, sir," said Daniel, miserably. It was one thing to know, oneself, that one had done wrong or been foolish; it was quite something else to be told this. If he hadn't been in the mess he was in, Daniel was certain he'd have answered back at this point. Daniel had a temper. Luckily, he also had good sense.

"Do you know why drink is so awful?" continued the eagle.

"No, sir."

"It makes cruel people worse. You look at the man, or woman for that matter, who habitually torments his dog, or his cow, or his child. Filled with drink they're ten times worse than when they're sober, and when they're sober they're the Devil himself. Wouldn't you agree?"

"Yes, sir," said Daniel. Privately, he thought, no, I don't agree. In his own case, drink brought out the best in him. It made him happy, it improved his dancing, and it enabled him to see beauty.

"Of course," the eagle continued in a lordly voice, "as you are a man of fairly good character, you don't get evil when you drink, you just become more witless than you normally are."

"Yes." (Daniel wasn't going to say "sir" or "your honour" any more; he was now irritated.)

"So, you do agree?"

"Yes," he said, quite quietly.

"Say it again so I can be sure I heard you right."

Perhaps, Daniel thought, this was the Devil disguised as an eagle. Anyway, he needed to tell him what he wanted to hear.

"Oh yes," replied Daniel, with little enthusiasm. "I do agree with you."

"When you drink, you become an idiot. Go on, say it."

"When I drink I become an idiot," Daniel admitted, churlishly.

"Will you promise me then," the eagle continued, now in a gentle, rather reasonable voice, "never to take another drink?"

A teetotal eagle, Daniel thought. What a truly amazing creature. "Oh yes, sir," said Daniel, quickly. "I will never drink again."

"You're not just lying in order to please me, are you?"

"Oh no," replied Daniel, and then he added, "sir," for effect.

"How do I know you're not lying? Men are always lying, aren't they?"

"Oh, but I'm not, I promise," said Daniel emphatically.

"You promise?"

"Oh yes."

"You're a man of your word, are you?"

"Oh, yes."

"And will you cross your heart?"

"Oh, yes. I cross my heart and hope to die if I ever drink again." He made the sign of the cross on his heart. The eagle slipped behind Daniel and reappeared in front of him a few moments later. Why the endless circling? Was it nerves? Hardly. Fear of Daniel? Impossible. So why?

"I suppose you're a decent enough man," said the eagle, finally, and disappeared again.

His entire future, Daniel realised, depended on what he said next. "I hope I'm decent," he said, sheepishly, when the eagle appeared in view again. "I'd like to think I was decent, anyway . . ."

"I don't remember you throwing stones at me or mine . . ." mused the eagle, and with that he was gone again.

So that was where the conversation was leading, thought Daniel.

"Oh no, sir," he agreed heartily, "I would never throw stones or do anything like that, never . . ."

"Or rob our nests or steal our eggs?" added the eagle from behind him.

In fact, Daniel had robbed many a bird's nest including those of one or two eagles. But he was a boy then, and what did boys know?

"Certainly not," he protested, as the eagle came into view again. "I'd never touch an egg in a nest, especially a nest of yours. I never have and I never will."

"All right," said the eagle, flapping his wings and rising into the air. "I like you enough, I think. More importantly, I believe you. Get up on my back. Get a good grip of my feathers so you won't fall off, and I'll fly you out of this bog."

"Your honour, you're making fun of me. Who ever heard of a man riding on an eagle like it was a horse?"

"It was never done before," the eagle agreed, "but so what? My offer is sincere. Climb on my back and I'll take you out of here. Or stay in this bog and starve. You choose. You could try and swim across Lough Dunne to the mainland but I don't think you'll make it. You're too cold, too tired and too drunk. And by the way, the stone you're on . . ."

"Yes," said Daniel.

"It's sinking under your weight, Daniel."

Daniel looked down. It was true. The stone was going and a peaty soup had spread around his feet. He jumped up and made for a clump of gorse. He wanted to clean the mess off his boots.

"You need my help," said the eagle, still circling him, "if you want to get out of here."

Daniel said nothing. Something was troubling him that he couldn't put into words. He began to wipe his boot soles on the wiry plant. He heard a slurping noise behind. He turned, just in time to see his stone seat sink beneath the surface.

Daniel realised that when night fell, he'd have fallen asleep on the stone; they'd have disappeared into the sludge together, and that would have been the end of him.

"Hurry up and decide will you," demanded the eagle, "I haven't all day."

By temperament, Daniel was conservative. Swimming was appealing because it was what he knew. Flying was not because it was what he didn't know. And Daniel didn't much care for heights, either. On the other hand, it was some way to the shore. The ground might split open as he walked there.

"Well, nothing ventured, nothing gained. I thank you for your offer, your honour, and I accept."

The eagle bounded towards him. "I can't stop properly, Daniel, in case the ground splits, so hop up quickly as I pass."

Daniel grabbed at the feathers on the eagle's upper neck. Then he half-jumped and half-hauled himself upwards. Suddenly, without his being quite aware just exactly how, Daniel was up on the eagle's back, his head buried in the bird's neck. The eagle smelt of egg, dust, straw, meal and meat. Geese had the same smell.

Daniel dropped his legs down as if he was riding a horse and, at the same time, he sat up. The moon was still high in the sky and its cold white light illuminated everything around.

He looked down and saw the brown ground with the slit through which the stone had fallen.

As the eagle rose higher, he saw the entire island. It was round and brown, with patches of purple heather and yellow gorse growing here and there. He saw the island's muddy shore. He saw the lead-coloured waters of Lough Dunne. The wind, blowing in his face, carried away the acrid smell of eagle, and brought to him a clean smell of mist and wet stone. Wisps of cloud floated past.

The eagle went on soaring upwards, as well as flying forwards. Now Daniel saw the River Dunne, and the ford where he had fallen. The cloud wisps were growing thicker.

Next, Daniel saw Reeky Hall. Megan was inside, he thought, bent over a fire, a smudge of soot on her lovely nose. He saw a man-servant carrying a creel of turf towards the kitchens.

"Well, you've hit the spot rightly, sir," said Daniel. "Now you can put me down anywhere here. Anywhere at all."

But the eagle went on and up to where the cloud got

thicker still. Did he hear me, wondered Daniel? He saw the estate schoolroom where he had danced and drank whiskey. He saw the stable block. He saw the sloping roof under which he slept. The blue-black slates of the roof, wet with dew in the moonlight.

He imagined his bed, his straw mattress, his goose-down bolster. How nice, he thought, to slide under the blankets and drift off to sleep with the familiar smell of leather wafting up from the tack room below.

"That's where I sleep," Daniel shouted. "Put me down anywhere and I can walk the rest. I don't want you to go to any more trouble, your honour."

But the eagle just went up and on to where the cloud was heavier still.

"Excuse me, can you hear me?"

Apparently not, Daniel thought, gloomily. The eagle went on climbing.

"I think we've overshot," suggested Daniel politely, "but it doesn't matter. I'm more than happy to get off any-where."

"Oh, I'd have thought a game young fellow like you would have wanted to see the world?" The eagle's tone was quite unpleasant.

"Of course, I'm very obliged to you for the ride," Daniel replied, quite emphatically. "I've enjoyed it. I've seen some wonderful sights. But now, please, put me down. I want to go home." For the first time, Daniel felt a faint trickle of anxiety.

"Oh, do you now?" said the eagle with mock-incredulity. "You want to go home?"

"Yes. Put me down anywhere, anywhere at all." Daniel was as forceful as he dared to be without causing offence.

"But sure if you've come this far with me, you might as well see the world." The eagle's tone was absolutely mocking now.

"I don't want to see the rest of the world," said Daniel.

"Oh, yes you do."

"No, I don't."

"Oh dear, lost our courage have we? Feeling nervous? Or did we drink too much last night and are we now feeling the worse for wear?"

"I want to go home."

"Didn't your mother ever tell you, don't look a gift horse in the mouth? How often do you get the chance to fly on an eagle's back? Never, I'd say. So sit back, enjoy the ride while it lasts."

"It's certainly true this is a great privilege," Daniel agreed, hoping this would mollify the eagle, "but all the same, if you don't mind, I still want to go home."

"I'm afraid the answer's no. I'm not going to let you throw away the chance of a lifetime. I shall show you the world, whether you like it or not, and in years to come you'll thank me for it."

The eagle soared on and up. The land gave way to a great greeny-grey sheet with white patches dabbed on it everywhere. This was the sea. After a while, the sea ended and everything below was green and brown again. Straight ahead, he saw the pale line of the horizon with the light of the rising, but still hidden, sun seeping over the top. They were going east, he thought, in which case it was the island of Britain that he saw below.

Now the cloud mist began to swirl about him in earnest; the higher the eagle climbed, the thicker and heavier it became.

Then, suddenly, the ground vanished from sight, and below him, all Daniel could see was a bumpy carpet of mist. He looked ahead. He was now inside a cloud. He saw his hands, each holding a clump of feathers; he saw the rounded back of the eagle's head; and he saw the front edge of the eagle's sharp beak.

This was no tour of the earth, Daniel realised. The eagle's intentions were unpleasant, malevolent even. He flew out of the cloud and Daniel was relieved to see the earth again.

"Where are you taking me, sir?" he asked, bleakly.

"Where am I taking you? Oh, I'm taking you on a little journey, Dan." His voice was now very chilly and un-friendly. "But don't you worry your pretty little head about it."

"Why don't you tell me where you're going? You do know where you're going, don't you?"

"You think I'd set off, willy-nilly, with no idea of where I was headed?"

"No." Daniel felt as he used to at school when a teacher forced him to admit something he didn't care to.

"I know exactly where I'm going."

"Well then, why don't you tell me? It's cruel not to tell someone where you're taking them. And as I never harmed you, you owe me that, at least."

"Yes, it is cruel, but then . . . I am cruel. I want you to panic. Can you manage that, Dan? Can you get your heart to speed up and your palms to sweat? I hope so. It would really cheer me up no end, if you could manage it."

The full awfulness of what was happening now began to bear in on Daniel. As a punishment for something – though he didn't know what – he was being taken somewhere – though he didn't know where. Probably somewhere truly dire, a desert say, full of lions and rats and cockroaches, where he would be abandoned and be eaten by wild animals. Or perhaps the eagle would go as high as he could and then he would tip Daniel off his back. Or perhaps the eagle would eventually reach the kingdom where only eagles lived; here, Daniel would be tried (the trial would be a farce); he would be found guilty; and then he would be pecked to death.

"You tricked me," protested Daniel hopelessly.

"Yes, I did, and it wasn't hard," the eagle replied. He sounded uncommonly cheerful.

"Why's that?" Daniel knew it was far better to talk than to imagine his fate.

"It wasn't hard because you're unbelievably stupid.

That's what never ceases to amaze me about ones like you. You obligingly dig your own hole in the ground and then you fall into it."

"You're talking in riddles," Daniel said.

"Yes, I suppose I am. Another sign of your colossal stupidity is that you can't work any of it out. But then, in my experience all your kind are stupid."

It was the intonation of the word "kind" that Daniel particularly noticed. Daniel remembered what the eagle said earlier; "I don't remember you throwing stones at me or mine. Or robbing our nests and stealing our eggs." Daniel had of course done both but he had denied it and had assumed the eagle had accepted what he said. This was arrogance – he saw that now. He must have hurt this eagle, or this eagle's relatives or friends. And now he was about to be punished.

Oh, he was a fool. Daniel felt colossal anger, partly with the eagle, but mostly with himself for being caught like this.

It was the whiskey, of course, Daniel concluded sadly. If he survived, he must never drink again . . .

Daniel blinked. There was no point thinking any more. He must turn away from himself and out to the world. Otherwise, his mood of despair would get worse and worse.

As the eagle moved forward and more cloud streamed past, Daniel kept thinking he might get something in his eye. But clouds were only vapour. When he finally understood this, he was able to stare ahead without flinching.

His impression, then, was of teased wool. It looked solid enough but had he reached out, he'd have grasped nothing but air. At least that was *one* thing that he did know for certain.

The eagle was still climbing steadily. After a while, Daniel sensed light coming down from above. It was whiter than sunshine but not as strong. Any moment now, he guessed, they would leave the cloud and ascend into the upper sky.

He was right. Suddenly, Daniel found himself in a cold, empty place with no cloud. He saw stars in the sky above, and the moon ahead. It was just the same as when he saw it from the schoolroom; it had the same shadows on the surface, that is. But it was much smaller close to than he would ever have imagined on earth, and it was also much brighter, which he would never have guessed either.

The glare made his eyes water. He glanced down and blinked. Suddenly, through the gaps in the clouds, he saw the earth; it was very small and round, and it was mostly blue or white with patches of brown here and there. It looked like a ball of different coloured waxes all scrunched together.

He wondered, was this what the Almighty saw? It was a thought he decided not to pursue. God always put him in mind of judgement and that, inevitably, led Daniel back to himself. Daniel had no doubt God existed, nor did he doubt that when God finally got His hands on Daniel, God would not be slow to show how displeased He was with Daniel and the life he had led. But that was ahead of him, years away, decades away, maybe; he was still a young man. Turn your face to the world, he told himself. And whatever you do, don't think . . .

He looked back at the moon. It was a couple of hundred feet away now. Again he saw its familiar smudges and its dips and hollows. He also saw there was a reaping-hook. The point was dug into the moon's surface and the handle stuck up into the air. It was on the left hand side, somewhere near the top.

For a moment Daniel was puzzled, and then he was exhilarated. So he had been right, earlier.

"Dan," the eagle said, suddenly.

"Yes," Daniel replied, wondering what next.

"I'm very very tired, you know. Why did you make me come all this way?"

"I didn't make you come all this way," said Daniel, puzzled.

"Yes, you did."

"I asked to get off at Reeky Hall but you ignored me."

"Oh, did I?" said the eagle meekly. "Maybe I did."

"You most certainly did. I pleaded, I begged, but you just flew on up into the sky. You were the one who wanted to come up here. I told you I wanted to get off. But would you listen? Oh no!"

"All right, if you say so," the eagle conceded, which

puzzled Daniel even more. Then the eagle sighed. "I'm so exhausted, I can hardly go on."

"Ah." Nervously, Daniel glanced sideways to check on the wings. He saw them rise and then fall and then rise again. More slowly than before? How could he judge?

Oh dear, if the eagle stopped beating his wings, then presumably he and the eagle would tumble back to earth, and Daniel would break into so many pieces, there would be none of him left.

"What are you going to do?" Daniel asked quietly.

"I'm going to have a little rest there on the moon."

"I see. And what are you going to do after you've had your rest?"

"We'll go back."

"To Reeky Hall?" said Daniel quickly.

"Oh yes," replied the eagle, blandly. "This adventure has definitely lost its lustre as far as I'm concerned."

He must be really worn out, thought Daniel. That was why he was acting like a befuddled old man.

"This is what we're going to do now," said the eagle, very pleasantly.

"Yes," said Daniel. Oh dear, he thought. The rise and fall of the wings was definitely getting slower and slower.

"You see that reaping-hook?"

"I do."

"When I pass by, you get hold of it and jump off. Can you do that?"

"All right."

"Sit down on the moon and stay there."

"All right. And what are you going to do?"

"I'm going to flop down on the top of the moon. I'll have a rest, get my strength back. Then I'll come back for you, and we'll fly back home."

"I like the sound of this plan," said Daniel.

"Ready," said the eagle.

"Yes," said Daniel.

The handle of the reaping-hook wasn't more than a dozen feet away. Daniel spat on his palms and reached into the air. A second or two later, he felt the smooth cold wooden shaft. He closed his fingers around it quickly. The eagle hovered and Daniel jumped sideways. His boot made a smacking noise as he landed on the moon. The eagle flew off.

Daniel found himself on a sharply curving slope. Holding tightly on to the shaft, he half-walked, half-scrambled up the side. The ground, though it looked like powdered chalk from far off, was in fact hard and bumpy and easy to walk on.

When he got above the shaft, Daniel sat himself down but he kept his feet resting on the shaft. Otherwise he'd have either slid down or worse, fallen off. Thank God for that reaping-hook, he thought, it must have been put there in order to give visitors something to hold on to. He decided it must be the eagle's doing.

"Mr Eagle," Daniel called, "where are you?"

Daniel heard the flapping of wings. The eagle came out from behind the moon and flew slowly past.

"I thought you said you needed a rest?"

"Well, you thought wrong."

"But you said you did."

"You're even more stupid than I guessed." His nasty tone had returned. The eagle vanished behind the moon. "I'm not tired," he continued. "Didn't you know eagles can fly their whole lives without ever stopping?"

"No," said Daniel. He felt sickened, depressed. He looked away. The sky was black with stars scattered across it. The horizon was blue. The sun was still out of sight. The earth was a tiny ball in the distance.

"Nice view, isn't it?" said the eagle when he re-appeared.

Daniel decided to ignore this remark.

"Oh dear. Lost our tongue, have we?"

Daniel glowered at the eagle.

"Well, I'm off. Enjoy the view, won't you. And enjoy the rest of your life."

He disappeared, then reappeared.

"Where are you going?" asked Daniel.

"Back to Reeky Hall."

"And I'm not coming?"

"That's the first intelligent statement I've heard you make."

The eagle went behind the moon again but his voice carried clearly to Daniel.

"Without water, I imagine you'll last about three

days. But before you die, think about this."

The eagle re-appeared and turned. Floating half-a-dozen feet away, he stared at Daniel with his dark black eyes.

"You robbed my nest. You robbed my mother's nest. And you robbed my mother's mother's nest. You killed my brothers and sisters and why you didn't kill me is a miracle. And now I'm going to kill you. You're the worst stealer of bird's eggs in the whole of Ireland, Daniel O'Rourke. When I saw you stranded on that miserable island, I had thought that I'd kill you quickly. But then, as I swooped down towards you, I thought, no; I'm going to arrange things so he takes a long, long time to die, in order that he can have plenty of time to contemplate his horrible crimes before he breathes his last breath."

Daniel felt in his pockets. He hoped to find something with which to hit the wretched eagle in the eye. He found only a clay pipe broken in two. It wasn't heavy enough. He would have to rely on his tongue.

"I should have smashed the egg you were growing inside and I wish I had. And if I had my life all over again, I'd make it my business to find every eagle's nest in the country and smash every egg I could lay my hands on."

"Well, how will you do that? Are you going to come back from the dead?"

"I hate you, you mean miserable trickster," Daniel shouted.

"Let me paint you a picture," said the eagle smugly, "of what's going to happen. You're either going to fall asleep and tumble back to earth and smash to atoms; or, you're just going to die of thirst and hunger and tumble to earth and smash to atoms. Either way, you're finished, and whatever happens, you deserve it."

The eagle spread his wings and began to laugh. At the same time, he dropped away like a stone.

"You blackguard," Daniel shouted.

What do I do now, Daniel wondered? He fancied a smoke but of course, apart from the fact that his clay pipe was broken in two, he had no way of lighting the tobacco in the bowl.

Maybe there was a fire on the moon, he thought hopefully. No, it was just a dusty white ball with dips it.

Well, this was a fine mess he'd got himself into. Oh yes. But he mustn't pursue that line. He must *do* something. He could still whistle, couldn't he.

He put his lips together and began to whistle "The Rakes of Mallow." It was a nice jaunty tune. He felt his spirits rising. Oh yes, this is the life. Listening to this lovely tune and looking down on the Earth. He was the only man, perhaps, in the whole history of the world, to have done this. He began to drum with his hands on his thighs and to tap with his boots on the shaft of the reaping-hook.

"Ya – hoo," he cried, "ya – hoo."

"What on earth is that horrible racket?" said a voice.

What was that? The eagle? No, this was an old voice. It cracked and warbled.

Daniel looked left and right, saw nothing. No one at all. Was he hearing things now?

"Who's that?" he shouted. His voice trembled slightly.

"What on earth's that horrible noise, I said," the cracking voice replied. "And when I ask a question, I expect an answer."

There was an awful sound of bolts drawing. Dry hinges with no grease on them began to squeal. Then a door – cut out of the surface of the moon and invisible until this moment – began to open. It was swung right back and fell with a clunk on the ground. An old man stood in the open doorway. He had a long dirty yellow beard. He wore a dark blue gabardine and green fingerless mittens. His eyes were bright and blue. They gleamed almost as brightly as the stars.

"Who are you?" asked Daniel.

"Who am I? Don't you know who I am? I'm the man in the moon."

The man stepped out of the door. He wore slippers with toes that curled up at the front. He was about three foot high.

"And you're Daniel O'Rourke, aren't you?"

"Yes, sir," said Daniel, amazed and confounded. "And how do you know me?"

"Oh, I know you. You're the biggest stealer of birds' eggs on the whole of the island of Ireland."

Daniel wondered whether to deny this. He decided this time better not.

"How do you know that?" he asked. Maybe he could talk his way out.

"Oh, stop asking questions," said the man. "You're not entitled to ask questions."

"Aren't I?" Daniel said mildly. He was intent on keeping this pleasant.

"Certainly not," said the man, crossly. "You're a visitor. Visitors answer questions. Otherwise they keep their mouths shut. Do you understand?"

What a grumpy old man, Daniel thought, but he said, "Yes, sir," very pleasantly.

The old man blew his nose on a blue handkerchief, put the handkerchief away and quickly moved two steps forward. He was nimble on his pins.

"How did you get here?" the man asked.

"Well, sir, I was on the way to Mrs Hardigan's. At Knowles's ford I chanced to look up at the beautiful night sky with the great jewel of the moon in the middle, and didn't I step right into the river. I was carried downstream, out into Lough Dunne. Here I chanced upon an island. Oh, it was a bleak, boggy miserable place and I haven't the name of it now."

"That'll be Pirate Island," said the man.

"Oh, thank you, your honour. It was a long way from the shore, too, and I didn't know how I was going to swim across, when down came the eagle. He offered to fly me home. I thought, why not. I hopped up on his back and off we went. But he was a trickster. I think I interfered with the nest he came from and since that day he's had a grudge against me. Of course I was a boy when I erred. I know better now, your honour. I swear I'd never do anything like it today. I tried to tell that eagle but he was deaf to my words. He turned away and dropped like a stone back to earth, and he left me here, where you see me now, sitting and wondering what to do next."

Daniel wondered if he could squeeze a tear out of his eye. He blinked a few times, just like he did when he was a boy. He really did feel pity, although only for himself. He dragged the corner of his sleeve across his face, and slyly glanced sideways at the same time. It was important the old man saw his tears. To his surprise, he saw the old man was smiling.

"So you fell for the oldest trick in the book? You got down from his back to give him a rest." The man was laughing now.

"Yes, sir," Daniel answered, slowly. How extraordinary that he should find this amusing.

The chuckling stopped. "By God, I'll pull that old eagle's feathers if I ever get hold of him."

"Is he coming back then?" Daniel made a big effort not to sound too bright or hopeful.

"How do I know?" said the old man bluntly. "When you get to my age, you know better than to bank on anything."

He stared into the distance and absent-mindedly unbuttoned his gabardine.

"The only thing you can ever be certain of is disappointment. You're always going to disappoint and be disappointed. Oh, yes, when He made the world He made certain there was more than plenty of that. Everyone could have as many helpings of disappointment as they wanted."

The coat fell open. The old man wore underneath an unexpectedly elegant waistcoat of black moleskin with red piping along the edges.

"That's why I live up here. I'll never be a disappointment to anyone. And I'll never be disappointed."

He fished in a pocket, pulled out a silver snuffbox and opened it.

"Death too. That's the other certainty. Did I mention that? You don't take snuff, do you?"

Unfortunately, before Daniel had a chance to say yes the old man said, "No, of course you don't. Nest robbers don't take snuff as a rule."

"Umh, I do," said Daniel quietly.

The man ignored him or else he didn't hear. He nipped a pinch of the brown powder between forefinger and thumb, lifted his fingers to his nose and breathed in, hard. He repeated the process with the other nostril. Then, as he pulled his handkerchief out of his pocket, he sneezed, hugely, and two great pieces of brown coloured mucus – they reminded Daniel of earthworms – flew out of his nose and landed on the cloth.

"Ah, that's better," he said, contemplating what lay on

his handkerchief and smiling. "That's better."

"Umh, I'm not averse to a bit of snuff you know," pleaded Daniel.

"Don't be ridiculous," said the old man. "I have to send to Jermyn Street in London for this. It's far too good for the likes of you." He put the snuffbox back in the pocket it came from.

"So, what do you propose to do now?" he asked.

"Propose," said Daniel. "How do you mean propose?"

"You know, what are you going to do next?"

"I don't know, sir." Actually, why not give him the truth? "I'm going to do nothing, sir."

"Nothing!" thundered the old man. "Nothing! That's preposterous. You must do something."

"What can I do?"

"Well, you must leave here, that's obvious."

"Leave?"

"Yes, leave."

"Oh, but I can't."

"Yes, you can."

"But I can't – how can I?"

"You should have made arrangements with the eagle," said the old man.

"I did, but then he broke his word and flew off."

"That's your lookout."

"That's true – but it's not my fault either. How did I know he was a trickster?"

"Everyone in the world does and if you didn't, you're

even more stupid than I thought. Anyway, you got on his back – you admit that?"

"Yes," Daniel agreed.

"And then you got off his back, yes?"

"Yes."

"So it is your fault, Daniel O'Rourke. See, you've admitted it. Take responsibility for your actions."

"You twist everything I say to make it seem like something else."

"I don't think so. Having admitted it's all your fault, it must be down to you do something about it."

"And what would that be?" asked Daniel.

"Well, leave."

"I can't leave . . . how can I leave . . . I can't fly home, can I?"

"Oh yes you most certainly can leave," the old man interrupted. "Go on, buzz off. This is my place. I don't want you here. Now, clear out."

"You'd actually kick me off the moon?"

"I most certainly would."

"And let me fall to my death?"

"I most certainly would."

"You wouldn't," Daniel exclaimed. "That would be . . . cold-blooded murder."

"You just watch. I can and I will. This is my moon. You're not welcome. Now, hop off, it's your last chance. Do what I say, or it'll be worse for you in the end, I promise."

"No, I won't," Daniel shouted. He slid down to the

shaft. Then he wrapped his legs around the bottom and his arms around the top. "You'll have to push me off yourself. And you wouldn't dare push a man off the moon to his death. You wouldn't dare, I know it."

"You just watch me." He looked like a man who was going to enjoy what he was about to do. No wonder he lived up here alone, thought Daniel. He wouldn't be welcome in Ireland or anywhere else.

The old man turned around and stepped nimbly towards his doorway, the tails of his gabardine wafting behind. He disappeared inside and from beyond the door came the unmistakable sound of drawers opening and closing.

Daniel heard footfalls and a cackle. He wrapped his arms and legs tighter around the shaft. The old man emerged from the doorway. He carried a very large cleaver. The blade was dull silver, the handle was yellow brown.

"Right, here we have the business. This is how we clear out trespassers. Watch out, Daniel O'Rourke."

The old man tripped towards him. Daniel considered. If he let go of the shaft and scrambled away, was it possible he could get to the top of the moon? And if he did get there, what then? He couldn't run down from his perch; he'd fall off. This really was the worst predicament he'd ever faced.

"Right, 'bye-bye, Mr O'Rourke. In future, don't impose where you're not wanted. It'll only lead to tears."

In one swift, single movement the little man crouched

down and swept the cleaver, sideways, along the surface of the moon. Fearing the blade would catch him on the side of his poor unfortunate feet, those whose ills, in a way, were the cause of all his misfortunes, Daniel instinctively lifted his legs out of the blade's way. This left the shaft of the reaping-hook bare and exposed.

The cleaver struck the wood just above the point where it emerged from the moon. It occurred to Daniel that this was what the old fellow intended all along – to cut him loose as opposed to cutting him with the blade. There was a sharp crack and Daniel knew the reaping-hook was cut in two.

A split second later Daniel fell forward and turned head-over-heels as he pitched off the moon. He saw, upside-down, the old man, cleaver in hand, waving.

"Goodbye, Daniel O'Rourke. Don't rob any more nests."

Then, still seen upside-down, he saw the old man stamp across the moon and disappear inside.

When he started to fall, Daniel was terrified. Then, as always in life, he grew accustomed to his situation. He saw he was going to die. He saw there was nothing he could do about it. He saw that he must turn his thoughts away from the present world. He saw, in a word, that he must say his prayers.

He moved his lips and mumbled, "Our Father, Who art in Heaven . . ."

He heard his voice as he started to speak and how

abnormally loud it sounded in the silence of space. Would he be heard? He doubted it. At that moment, as he fell, he was certain he was completely and utterly alone. Yet he said the words anyway, all the way to end. He said them out of habit; he said them to comfort himself; and he said them because he thought it was good insurance. If he had to face his maker, at least Daniel would have to his credit the fact he had prayed before his end. And if there was no maker, it wouldn't matter to Daniel; he'd be dead before he discovered the truth.

Daniel entered the clouds and sometimes he could see the moon and the earth, one shrinking, one expanding, and sometimes with the mist swirling around him, he was in an all-white-and-grey cloudy world, where he saw nothing but mist. He might almost have been underwater.

When Daniel came out of the clouds and into the sky that lay underneath, the world was much, much bigger. Soon he would strike the ground. He felt tears welling up in his eyes and trickling down his cheeks. He wished he'd led a better life. He wished he hadn't drunk whiskey the night before. He wished he'd married Megan and had a child. He wished he'd never said or done a hundred things, and he wished he'd done a thousand things. His thoughts, like his body, spun on and on, faster and faster, until at last, wiping his sleeves over his wet face, he told himself he had had his life. Regrets were useless. He must try to remain cheerful. He must make the best of his last few moments before what ever was going to happen next, happened.

And that was when Daniel heard it. It was an indecipherable noise, far away. But drawing closer, he realised what it was. It was the honking of geese.

He spun around and saw them, some way beneath him but directly in his path, seven fat white geese with long necks and yellow beaks, slowly beating their wings as they flew through the air.

My goodness me, Daniel thought, perhaps they would help.

"Hello," Daniel called. "Can you help me?"

The geese beneath him turned their heads this way and that as they scanned the sky beside and beneath.

"Up here!" Daniel shouted. "Above you."

The large gander at the front tilted his long neck back and looked up. "What are you doing up there?" he asked.

My goodness, Daniel thought. From above, one goose looked just like any other. But the voice was distinct. Daniel knew it well. It was the gander of the flock who lived in the paddock at Reeky Hall. He was a big brute and, as geese went, he was not especially unpleasant or bad-tempered.

"Don't mind how I got here," Daniel shouted, "Will you help me?"

"I don't mind," replied the gander.

"Well, get underneath me, I'll land on your back."

"Is that a cudgel you're holding?" the gander called.

What was he on about? Daniel wondered. Then he realised.

198

"It's the handle of a reaping-hook," he explained. "Don't ask how I got it, it's too long a story."

The gander wheeled again. He was fifty, fifteen, five feet away . . . Then, with a resounding CAL-UMPH, Daniel felt his rump land on the broad, fatty, feathered back of the bird. A second after, he was pitched forward. He threw his arms around the gander's neck and his nose was buried in its down. It smelt vaguely of meal, mud and water. There was also that familiar smell of bird, sharp and acrid and metallic, the same smell the eagle gave off. Fortunately, it wasn't as pungent.

"Fallen far?" said the gander, blithely.

"Only from the moon," said Daniel.

"Oh. What were you doing up there?"

"Oh, nothing really."

"Hanging about?"

"Sort of."

"And how's himself?"

"You mean, him up there?" Oh dear. How should he answer? What if they were friends?

The gander continued, "He's a crotchety old devil, isn't he? The way he hisses and snarls at any one who comes within ten feet of his blessed moon, you'd think he was a goose in a previous life."

"Would you?" said Daniel, hoping that by being vague he would seem tactful. "I don't know." No point annoying this bird.

"So how did you get up there, anyway? It seems a very

long way to go for the handle of reaping-hook, if that's what you went for."

"It's a long story," said Daniel.

"It's a long flight," said the gander. "Gather round, girls." He flew more slowly so the other geese could gather round him.

"It's like this," began Daniel, and he told the entire story.

"That's a tale and a half," said the gander when he finished.

"Are you planning to rob any more nests?" asked one of the geese sharply.

"Oh no," Daniel protested, "never again."

"How do we know you won't rob any more nests?" she insisted.

"I'm telling you, I won't . . ."

"You say that but you look, to me, like a man who just says what he thinks others want to hear. Isn't that right, girls?"

The geese honked in agreement.

Daniel felt anxious. He was still some way from the ground. They could tip him off the gander's back if they took a notion. He looked about himself. He saw the ocean below and a ship moving across the surface.

"Oh look," exclaimed Daniel, "drop me down near her and I'll get a lift home."

"No, I'll take you there," said the gander, "I'm going that way."

"I'm a heavy weight," Daniel protested, "and it's a long road."

"He's a nest robber," said the same goose as had spoken before. She hissed, and with her long flat beak she bit Daniel sharply on his ankle.

"Yeow!" Daniel exclaimed, "that hurt." Without thinking what he was doing, he lashed at the bird with the shaft of the reaping hook. He hit her a nasty smack on the base of her neck.

"He hit me!" she squealed.

"He hit her," all the females squealed horribly and then hissed together. Daniel felt a beak snapping his knee, then a really nasty pinch on his free hand. He whacked the bird on her wing. She let go his hand and peeling sideways she screeched, "He's a robber of nests. He doesn't deserve to live."

"That's enough," he heard the gander call gruffly. "The eagle would rob our nests as easily and with as little conscience as Daniel here."

"Shame on you, shame on him," the voices round him chorused.

"Have it your way," said the gander, "what do I care?"

Daniel felt himself dropping away from the circle of geese. The gander was swooping towards the sea.

"You've offended them," the gander said, "and I don't mind saying they have a point. In the interests of peace, I'm going to drop you here. The sailors can take you ashore and you can make your way home then. By the time you're back in old Reeky, all this will be forgotten."

The gander tilted so that Daniel tumbled sideways and dropped through the air. He hit the ocean like a stone. Although the water broke his fall, it didn't stop it all together. Daniel began to sink. Oh no, next stop the ocean floor.

But at that moment a whale swam by, saw Daniel and opened his mouth. A moment later Daniel found himself inside the creature's stomach. It was filled with seaweed and dead fish and rocks, and a rowing-boat of all things.

Daniel and the whale started up a conversation. Daniel told his story, as you can imagine. The whale had often lain about the surface of the sea, looking up at the moon, so he found that part of the story particularly intriguing. As for the nest-robbing part, the whale didn't give a fig. He didn't care for birds and birds didn't care for him. He lived in the sea and they lived in the air.

Of course, if Daniel's journey had involved a whaling ship and a crew of whalers, and if Daniel had been sympathetic to these characters, that would have been a different story. The whale had nearly been caught and killed by whalers several times himself. And he had several harpoons, still stuck in his back, to prove it.

"That was a good tale," the whale said, when Daniel finished. "Where did you say you wanted to go?"

"The Kerry coast," said Daniel, and he added, "your honour."

"Anywhere in particular?"

"Anywhere at all will do."

"Well, if any place will do, here's the place for you."

The whale opened his mouth and vomited. Daniel had a confused sense of himself shooting through the water, with the rowing-boat, the rocks, the seaweed and everything else from the whale's stomach, tumbling around him . . .

"Wake up, will you, you drunken sot," he heard.

Daniel opened his eyes. He saw the old lined creased face of Megan, his wife of thirty-something years, looming above him. She was holding a wooden bucket with a leather handle. His face was wet. His shirt was wet. His collar was wet.

"Are you awake?" Megan shouted down at him.

She tipped the bucket and another splash of water tipped into his face.

"Of course I'm awake," Daniel spluttered. "What did you splash me for the second time, you old witch, when you saw I was already awake?"

"You deserved that second splash because you're a drunken fool who's fallen asleep in the last place he should ever fall asleep," she exclaimed.

"And where's that?" Daniel asked, groggily. He shook his head and looked around.

"You're in the middle of Dullaveen Court," she said, "and you're lying right on the fairy stone."

Daniel looked round. It was true. He was sitting on the

fairy stone – it was a large square boulder – and ringed about him were a perfect circle of beech, oak and ash trees. He was in Dullaveen Court, supposedly owned by the fairies.

"I've had the strangest night," said Daniel.

"Have you now. I'll warrant you have. So did I," said Megan. "When you didn't come home from the public house, like you said you would, like you always do, and I always believe you too because I'm a fool, I waited up by the fire. And then, when it was first light outside our little windows, I said to myself, he's got drunk and he's sleeping it off somewhere. I'd better go and find him in case he's unconscious in the middle of the post road and the Dublin Mail comes along and the driver doesn't see him and the wheels of the coach cut my Daniel in two.

"So off I set, taking my bucket with me, thinking I'll get water from the well on the way back. And on the road, I met one neighbour after another, and to each one I said, 'Have you seen my Daniel? Have you seen Daniel? he didn't come home last night, you see.'

"And then at last I met that nasty toper, Brendan whatever-his-name is, and he says, 'Ah, yes, Mr O'Rourke, I saw him last night heading for the fairy fort.' You'd been dared, said Brendan, by your pals, to spend the night in Dullaveen Court, and if you lived to tell the tale, said Brendan, they'd all have to stand you a drink in the pub the next night. And if you died, they'd all toast your corpse at your wake.

"'Ah ha,' I said, when I get this information. 'Spent the night in the fairy fort did he? Spent the night up there in a drunken stupor, did he? And me sitting at home by the fire, fretting and worrying. Well, I'll give him a drink he won't forget in a hurry.'

"I filled my bucket at the well and I climbed up here and I found you, just like Brendan said I would, snorting and snoring like a pig on the fairy stone. And I tipped the bucket over you and gave you the first half of your glass. And now you can have the rest of it!"

As Megan went to tip the bucket, Daniel raised his arm, thinking he still had the shaft of the reaping hook and he could push her and the bucket away. But his hand was empty. Uselessly, he swiped the air with his arm. A gobbet of water came flying through the air and hit him full in the face.

He stood up, dripping. "You're a nasty mean-minded woman," he shouted.

"And you're a nasty mean-minded toper," Megan shouted back. Old Daniel took his handkerchief out of his pocket and mopped his face.

"Come here and I'll tell you what happened," said Daniel, putting the handkerchief away and starting towards the trees. Though it was gloomy inside the ring, he could tell that in the world outside, it was a bright summer's morning.

"I've been on the most marvellous journey," he said.

"You had evil dreams you mean," said Megan, "you should know that anyone who sleeps up here has evil dreams from the fairies."

"A dream . . . all right then, but it felt as real as that tree over there. And it wasn't all evil. For a start, I was young again. It was the night of the party in the school-room. Do you remember that, when Mr Savage came back from India, God rest his soul, with his bride, God rest her soul, and old Mr Savage, God rest his soul, do you remember . . . we were courting . . ."

"I think I can remember . . . just about," said Megan, grumpily.

There was no educating or improving the old blackguard, Megan thought. He'd drunk their money, and he'd slept the night in Dullaveen Court. Any other man would be ashamed of himself but not Daniel. When a man loved the bottle, as he did, he didn't behave or act like other men. Her life, at times, was miserable because she did not understand this.

"So," continued Daniel, "there I was, back in the school-room, the musicians were there, the Savages were there, you were there . . ."

The story, Megan thought grimly, what ever it was, would be all round Bantry by nightfall. She was right. For the next week, there was talk of nothing else, and whether he had dreamt it, or whether it was real, was the subject of lively debate for years afterwards.

I was the last to hear O'Rourke's famous tale. Two days after we spoke, he passed away. End of him, end of story.'

Part Seven

Inferno

Mr Cink sat back in his seat and smiled at his listeners. 'It has no moral,' he said, 'it's just a tale. And it has something for everyone, if I may say so. Even the boy.'

Mr Cink was staring at me. He was both trying to see what I thought and letting me know that I must choose him. He pointed at me. I felt my heart shrinking.

'Did you like it?' he asked. 'You're between friends. You can tell the truth.'

'Yes, sir,' I said. It was true, I had. But I had liked the first two stories as well. Now Mr Fee wasn't in the competition, but Mr Smyth was. What was I going to do? Mr Smyth's story and Mr Cink's story were as good as each other. I should never have agreed to be the judge. Especially with Mr Cink looking at me like he was. A story wasn't like a sum; a sum was either right or wrong. But a story could never be said to be right or wrong. I'd listened to each story and I thought they were each as good as each other because my attention hadn't strayed once.

'So, you've decided, haven't you? I'm the winner.' This was Mr Cink.

'I haven't decided,' I said.

'Oh, look, the sea,' said Mr Smyth, suddenly.

The train was sliding to a halt and there was the ocean.

'Where are we?' asked Mr Fee.

'Clew Bay,' I said.

'Nearly there.' Mr Fee took out his fob and squinted at the face. 'Yes, just a few minutes, gentleman, and we'll be at Achill. And I must say, thanks to you Mr Cink, the journey passed in the blink of an eye.'

'Yes,' agreed Mr Smyth, quietly, 'I don't think I noticed the train stopping at a single station. And now suddenly, here we are, almost there.'

It had been the same for me. I hadn't once thought about my work or the dining-car or Mr Cribben or anything. In my imagination, for the last few hours, I was either by the sea with Micky Mealiffe, or in the cow-house with Jeremiah O'Dwyer, or on the back of an eagle with Daniel O'Rourke. It was certainly the best run to Achill I'd ever had. Thank goodness the train was almost empty. I'd never have got the chance otherwise.

'Mr Smyth, I don't know why you're so surprised,' said Mr Cink. 'In the hands of a genius like myself, everything vanishes and the tale is everything. Of course you didn't notice the train stopping at one little miserable station after another. I had you spellbound, tranced. You were out of this world.'

'I include Mr Fee's in this. I thought his was marvellous too,' said Mr Smyth.

'I thought you just meant mine.'

'You do have a very high opinion of yourself, don't you?' said Mr Smyth.

'No, my opinion is perfectly objective,' said Mr Cink. 'Knowing how good I am, it follows it's perfectly reasonable to have the opinion I hold.'

'Archie,' said Mr Smyth, 'take him down a peg or two. Tell him my story is better than his!'

'I'm still trying to decide,' I said.

'Leave the judge alone,' said Mr Cink, 'stop interfering with him.'

There was a long pause. The train had stopped. The engine idled in the distance. I heard the sea. I felt sick.

'I can't decide,' I said, finally. 'I just can't.'

'Oh, all right then,' said Mr Cink, reasonably. 'We'll throw it open to chance. Why not? I might win, I might lose, I don't care. I'm a big man.'

He strode down the compartment to the door and flung it open.

'What are you doing?' Mr Fee exclaimed. 'You're only allowed to open the door at a station or in an emergency.'

'Shut up,' said Mr Cink.

Mr Cink jumped out and a crunching noise came back through the door. He'd landed on the edge of the bed of stones on which track rested.

'What if the train goes off?' said Mr Fee.

'It's not going to just "go off," like that,' said Mr Cink, sticking his head through the open door. 'It can't "go off" unless it's got up a head of steam, and that'll take it minutes which is plenty of time to climb aboard.'

'So, what's your plan?' asked Mr Smyth. 'How do you intend to settle the matter, out there?'

'Simple. I pick two stones from the millions littering the track, one white, one black. I put them in my deerstalker. Young Archie here puts his hand in the hat and picks out a stone. If he picks a white stone, then you're the winner, Mr Smyth, and of course, if he picks a black stone, why then I'm the winner. Is that fair?'

'Go on then,' Mr Smyth said, jerking his head at me, 'Go out and choose a white stone. But be sure to watch him, he's slippery.'

I ran down between the seats and jumped out through the door. I saw Mr Cink a couple of feet away. He had his back to me so he didn't think I could see. But I saw him pick first one and then a second black stone.

'Right, Archie, my boy, are you ready?' He straightened up and turned towards me. At the same time he dropped the two stones he had chosen into his deerstalker. There was a small hill right behind him with a circle of oaks on top, an old fairy fort of course, and because of where Mr Cink was in relation to the hill, it looked, as if the trees were a crown resting on his head. His eyes were now quite yellow.

I swallowed. 'Yes,' I said.

'If you pick me, Archie,' Mr Smyth called from the door, 'I will give you a guinea.'

'And I will give you a guinea as well,' Mr Fee added.

'I'm more generous. I'll give you ten.' Mr Cink proffered the deerstalker hat, shaking it at the same time so the two black stones inside clinked against each other.

I stretched my hand out. I didn't want Mr Cink to win. His story was neither better nor worse than Mr Smyth's, or Mr Fee's, but I wanted Mr Smyth to win. He was nice and Mr Cink wasn't.

But now Mr Smyth wouldn't win. Whichever stone I pulled out it would be black and Mr Cink would win.

'Hurry up, Archie.' The yellow eyes flashed at me.

I dropped my hand down. I felt the lining of the hat against my knuckles. What did I do? Take out both stones and drop them? Knock the hat to the ground and insist we start again . . . or did I? . . . And then suddenly I knew exactly, exactly what to do . . .

I took hold of a stone. As I lifted it out, I made as if to stumble. My hand flew forward and, an instant later, the stone clinked on the ground and was gone.

'Never mind,' I said, and my hand went straight back into the hat and grabbed the other stone.

'There are stones everywhere,' I said quickly, 'we'll never find the one I dropped. But from whatever this is, we'll know what that was.'

I saw Mr Cink staring furiously at me. The colour of his eyes had changed from yellow to black. I opened my palm.

'It's black,' I said, joyfully. 'You win, Mr Smyth.'

Before Mr Smyth had a chance to even smile, a ferocious wind suddenly blew past. I felt as if an enormous hand had swiped me, very hard, from behind. My hat was lifted from my head and blown into the air.

'You wretched child,' shouted Mr Cink. He was ten foot high, suddenly, and growing.

He reached with a fist towards my face.

'I'll rip your head off,' he said.

I darted round him, and began to run down the side of the train. 'Help, help,' I shouted, and I banged on the sides of the carriages I passed. I kept looking up at the windows at the same time. Someone would see me surely. Someone would open a door and yank me up on to the train.

But I didn't see anybody looking out. And no one opened a door and pulled me aboard.

I shouted, 'Mr Cribben, Mr Cribben,' as I approached the dining-car. But Mr Cribben wasn't there. No one was there. There was no one on the train. The engine, I thought, the driver, the stoker, they'll save me.

But when I got to the engine, I found no one aboard.

Then I heard the explosion. A huge pillar of black smoke roared out of a first-class carriage. It was coming from our compartment if I wasn't mistaken.

I turned again and I ran along the rails, and I didn't stop until I got to Mallaranny, the last station before Achill.

'What's up, Archie?' asked the stationmaster when I appeared, red-faced and breathless.

I pointed down the track at the train but I couldn't explain. The stationmaster sent word to the barracks. A few minutes later a sergeant with a young constable appeared, both carrying rifles on their shoulders.

I walked back to the train with them. It was exactly as I had left it, the engine steaming quietly, the carriages lined up behind.

We climbed aboard and began to make our way down the train.

'Where is everybody?' said the sergeant. 'It's absolutely empty, completely deserted. It's extraordinary.'

'And this was where we were,' I said, when we reached the compartment, 'me and the three men.'

The sergeant opened the door and we all stepped inside. Every surface was covered with thick black soot. Mr Cink's luggage was gone. There was a smell of burnt meat. A boot stood on the floor smouldering. I recognised it as Mr Smyth's.

The constable walked across to the open door on the other side, the one I'd jumped out.

'Sergeant,' he said.

The sergeant followed him over, I followed the sergeant and we all looked out.

There was a fire burning up among the fairy ring of trees on the hill and smoke floated into the air.

'Something wicked,' said the sergeant, 'this way comes . . .'

More police came. The train was searched. Mr Cribben,

the driver, the stoker and the conductor, as well as Mr Fee, Mr Smyth and Mr Cink could not be located. They had vanished into thin air. No other passengers were found to be missing. When the train stopped at Clew Bay, apart from the MGWR employees, the only passengers aboard, it seemed, were Mr Fee, Mr Smyth and Mr Cink . . .

What happened? Who knows? I didn't grasp it then, and sixty years later, after having a lifetime to turn it over in my mind, I still don't.

For the very best in Irish writing,
look out for
the Green Mammoth logo!

Mammoth

If you enjoyed *Caught on a Train*,
you might also like these books by
the following top Irish writers.

Frozen Out

Carlo Gébler

Phoebe leaves London and everything she
has known to go and live with her family in
Northern Ireland. But soon there are new
friends, especially Emma, and there is
laughter. But then there is a betrayal . . .

Carlo Gébler has written a warm and deeply
moving story about confronting for the first
time the awful fact that friends can turn
against you.

Black Death

Herbie Brennan

After visiting Maris Caulfield, and ancient village
where every inhabitant died
from the plague, can Janie Hyde really
be haunted by one of its victims?
Is she losing her mind?

She couldn't be responsible for the pestilence
returning to contemporary Britain through
the ghost of one of its
very first sufferers. Or could she?

You just don't listen

Sam McBratney

'You're rubbing out every single thing I've grown up with. I'm not going.'

Sixteen-year-old Laura is devastated when she finds out that her widowed mother plans to move to the country. The discovery of a new man in her mother's life makes her even more determined to stay in the city she loves.

'Warm-hearted McBratney . . . has the gift to see the funny side of things without being unfair to the emotions of everyone involved.'
The Times

Funny, how the magic starts

Sam McBratney

Seymour Brolly is as odd as two left shoes.
He wears binoculars all the time, is never
afraid to speak his mind, starts a campaign to
save the blue whale by writing to the emperor
of Japan, and is determined to save the
sand martens from the hands of builders.

Monica is aghast to have him as a new
neighbour, especially when he develops a
crush on her and pays her brother for her
photo. But when Seymour takes a stand
against the builders, Monica is the only
one who supports him.

Funny, how the magic starts . . .

One Grand Sweet Song

Short stories
by
Sam McBratney

Life is full of good times and bad times,
of surprises and choices. Its variety is
explored in these special stories about times
past and times to come. Together they form
a collection to celebrate the richness of
life – 'one grand sweet song'.

Flame Angels

An anthology of Irish writing by
Dermot Bolger, Herbie Brennan, June Considine,
John McGahern, Marilyn McLaughlin,
Joseph O'Conner, David O'Doherty,
and Michael Tubridy, ed. Polly Nolan

Freak?

Flower child?

True believer?

Who are you?

Coming home?

Climbing mountains?

Where are you going?

Some of Ireland's best writers tell how the smallest
thing can change your life, for ever.

Josie

Dutch Cooper

Josie is raised in a town inhabited by
animals, who are loving parents and
adoring friends. When she grows up,
Josie marries her beloved soldier.

But all the while, the Tar Men, with
their chalk white faces, cast a disquieting
shadow over her life, invading her
dreams and threatening the happiness
of her family . . .

'Josie is warm, wise and lyrical, and like all
true fairytales, as familiar and disturbing
as a dream.' *Annie Dalton*

WORLD MAMMOTH

Greg

Dirk Walbrecker

Greg wakes up one morning to discover
he is a caterpillar. His brother Ben is
grossed out, Mum suggests herbal
remedies and Dad simply refuses to
accept the creature is his son.

Greg becomes used to an existence of
munching through vast quantities of
greenery and climbing walls and ceilings.
Then the media gets hold of his story and
'Greggy' becomes a TV star!

But for Greg the fame loses its gloss when
someone close betrays him . . .

WORLD MAMMOTH

Dreaming in Black and White

Reinhardt Jung

In his dreams, Hannes finds himself back
in 1930s Germany. He is persecuted by
his fellow pupils and teachers, for Hannes
is disabled and, like the Jews and 'social
misfits', the Nazis have labelled him
'not worth living'.

He finds solace in the love of his mother
and Hilde, a Jewish friend. But what of
his father? Has he begun to believe the
Nazi propaganda?

'An utterly compelling, horrifyingly
credible account of how it was to be a child
in the Third Reich.' *Michael Morpurgo*

WORLD MAMMOTH